RITES

OF

PASSAGE

REST IN POWER NECROMANCY, PREQUEL

AMBER FISHER

D1082576

BOOKS IN THE REST IN POWER
NECROMANCY SERIES

OTHER BOOKS BY AMBER FISHER

MRS. LEWIS WAS DYING.

The lights were dim, and soft music drifted from a stereo. Three generations stood around the bed, her youngest daughter, Eloise, crying softly on her brother's shoulder. Another daughter, Beth, sat at her side, holding her hand and gently stroking the old, weathered skin. Every once in a while, someone uttered a small comfort, saying things like "Everything is okay" and "We love you."

They were doing and saying all the right things; they'd been diligent in studying their end-of-life care manual. I took a bit of pride in that. Over the past few weeks, I had met often with this family, preparing them for exactly this moment. Mrs. Lewis had been with us for four months, and today would probably be her last night at the hospice. Everyone was here.

Well, almost everyone.

"Where's Jessica now?" It was her son, Jim, who asked.

Beth whipped out a phone, tapping it a few times before answering. "She's still almost 45 minutes away." She cursed, anger flashing over her face before she composed herself, taking in a slow, deep breath and breathing it out in a long, controlled exhale. I taught her that trick, too. The energies surrounding the dying needed to be calm. No anger. Beth looked like she was doing her best.

"I don't think we have that long," Eloise said, fresh tears forming in her eyes. "What are we going to do if she can't make it?"

Jim frowned, his expression incredulous. "What kind of question is that? There's nothing we *can* do. If she makes it, great. But if she doesn't…" Jim gave an impotent shrug. "She knew the risks when she went out of town."

The tension in the air grew thicker; it wasn't unusual for this to happen, especially when death was close and someone important was absent. The moments before death were already such a fraught time, and everyone wanted them to be perfect. Not just for the dying, but for themselves. *Mostly* for themselves. They wanted to look back on this moment and know they did everything right—said the right things, cried the right way. They wanted this final punctuation mark at the end of a lifelong sentence to be exactly right.

But it rarely was.

In her bed, Mrs. Lewis shifted. She'd been so still for the past several hours that her movement drew everyone's attention. She was struggling to sit up. I leaned forward, observing her closely. Sometimes, when the old people were close to death, they asked to go home. They'd try to get out of their beds, but we couldn't let them, and that clash of intentions was always hard for everyone. Eloise had asked me here to help them through this transition and to intervene if necessary. Although this family knew what to do in theory, none of them were really ready.

But then, they never are.

Mrs. Lewis's gaze turned away from her family, towards the window. Her breathing was slow and noisy; the adults in the room grimaced as her chest rattled in time with the humming of the air conditioner. Though I'd worked in hospice for a long time now, even I found the death rattle disturbing.

As her gaze drifted away from her gathered family, Mrs. Lewis's expression began to change. She looked almost happy. Her eyes were lighting up, and she opened her mouth to speak. It took a moment to get her words out; her throat was too dry. Eloise offered her water, which she sipped absently, never taking her eyes off the window. When she finished, she pushed the water glass away.

"Jacob," she said, the slightest smile curving over her mouth. "I knew you'd be the first one I saw."

Eloise's gaze followed her mother's. "Mom?" Eloise said, a note of fear in her voice. "Mom, who are you talking to?"

Mrs. Lewis smiled as she nodded, ignoring her daughter's question. "I was always happy with you, Jacob. And soon enough we'll be happy together again."

Jim turned to me, his brow furrowed. "Is she hallucinating? You didn't say anything about hallucinating."

I considered the best way to answer this. Was Mrs. Lewis hallucinating? I didn't think so, but I couldn't say for sure. Because while I couldn't see ghosts, I could sense them. In that way, being a necromancer in the death care industry had its advantages. My inborn abilities made me sensitive to death and the death current, allowing me to sense death in many ways. Primarily, I could smell it. It smelled of Palo Santo, copal, and strangely, Lemon-scented Pledge furniture polish. But sometimes, when there's a ghost, I smelled other things, too. It varied from ghost to ghost, depending on the life the person led, their personality, how they smelled in life and probably many other things.

At that moment, I smelled Jacob Lewis's unique ghost smell. Menthol cigarettes. Lawn clippings. Aftershave. Motor oil.

I swallowed. "Is Jacob your father?"

Jim nodded. "He died about 10 years ago."

I nodded toward the window. "That may be, but he's here now."

Everyone in the room, except Mrs. Lewis, turned to me then, their expressions leaden, whether with fear or anger, it was hard to say. "Don't say that," snapped the eldest daughter, Beth. "This is hard enough as it is. No need scaring everybody half to death as well. There's no such thing as ghosts." She turned to one of the small boys, who whimpered and stuck a thumb in his mouth. "There's no such things as ghosts, sweetheart."

I turned my gaze away. There wasn't any point in arguing with her.

Mrs. Lewis was still addressing her dead husband. "Yes, I'm coming." She turned her gaze to Eloise. "Ellie, tell him I'm coming!"

At this, Beth pushed away from the bed. A steely determination replaced the sadness in her eyes as her nostrils flared and she headed toward the door. "I'm getting Camille," she said.

My breath caught in my throat. Mrs. Lewis hadn't asked for Camille, and there wasn't a good reason to disturb the room's vibe. Bringing in another person, even a nurse, was the wrong thing to do. This family knew that. I had taught them that.

But I wasn't family. I couldn't tell them no. I was here to

support, not to direct.

It was only a few moments before Beth returned to the room with Camille in tow. She glanced around the room and, when her gaze met mine, tendered a small smile, which I tried to return. It was unusual to have two death workers in the room at once, and I felt suddenly superfluous. I was only a certified nursing assistant; Camille was an actual nurse. I straightened my back and squared my shoulders, silently berating myself for my silly feelings of betrayal. This family wasn't loyal to me. We weren't friends. And anyway, there was no reason to get territorial.

There was always plenty of death to go around.

Camille took Beth's place at Mrs. Lewis's side. She placed her hand on the old woman's forearm and smiled. She was murmuring something too quiet for me to hear when the energy of the room changed.

My hands began to buzz as the energy slowed. I recognized that shift, and I swallowed, preparing myself for what I knew was coming next. The death current, the invisible force that moves through all living things, encouraging them to slow, decay, and eventually die, was ramping up. I felt it in my hands as a buzzing, and I sensed it with my nose. The aromas of incense and lemon grew thick. I took a step forward, my eyes glued to Mrs. Lewis's face.

A few moments passed before I felt the next change. The buzzing in my hands turned to a slow, cold throb, and I clenched my fists at my sides. This, too, was part of the dying process. The throbbing of my hands meant that Mrs. Lewis was now surrounded by mortic energy. Unlike the death current, which was always present everywhere, mortic energy only appeared at the moment of death, allowing the soul to slip from the body.

When mortic energy appeared, death was imminent. I held my breath.

Camille brushed a stray lock of hair from Mrs. Lewis's face. "Mrs. Lewis." Her voice was sweet and velvety, a throaty contralto. Camille's voice could charm a snake charmer. "Don't you want to stay with me a while?"

Hearing these words, my mouth fell open. What Mrs. Lewis *wanted* didn't matter; it was her time to go. The appearance of the mortic energy proved that. Of course, Camille couldn't sense mortic energy. Non-necromancers couldn't. Still, it wasn't right to give patients false hope that they could avoid death. Our job was to ease the transition, not ask them to fight it.

Camille knew this. So what was she doing?

I cleared my throat. "Camille? I wonder if—"

The nurse turned to me, her eyes bright even in the dimness. She smiled and tilted her head to one side. "Kezia? Would you mind stepping out of the room a moment, please?"

I balked. My gaze flit to Eloise, who had asked me to be here. The woman nodded her assent and I, feeling strangely embarrassed, headed toward the door.

But Mrs. Lewis's voice stopped me. "No," she said, "Jacob doesn't want Kezia to go."

Again, I looked to Eloise for direction. She hesitated this time, looking from me to Camille, whose sweet expression never changed. Finally, Eloise nodded once more.

"I'll be just outside in the hall if you need me," I said. I pushed open the door and left.

I only had to wait a minute or two before the door swung open and Camille stepped into the hallway, her expression serene. She patted me gently on the arm as she brushed passed me. "All better now," she said as she moved down the hall.

Confused, I stepped back into the room. The family's expressions had changed. They no longer looked afraid; now, they looked almost peaceful. It took me a moment to figure out why. When the realization struck me, I faltered.

My hands weren't buzzing. They didn't throb. And the death smells had lessened significantly. They never went away, not in a place like this. Death was always present if you knew where to look. But no longer were the death smells pressing.

I cast my gaze toward Mrs. Lewis, finding her still awake. Breathing. *Alive.*

But that was impossible. I'd felt the mortic energy in the room. And once mortic energy appeared, it didn't leave until the patient died.

But somehow, it was gone. Yet Mrs. Lewis remained.

What the hell had just happened?

"She won't die tonight," Eloise was saying as she sniffled and smiled, stroking her mother's cheek. "Jessica will get to see her and say goodbye." She laughed then, shaking her head in disbelief. "I swear, that woman must have a direct line to God," she said. "We only met Camille last week. She told us she could help if we needed her. But I never thought..." Again, she shook her head.

I looked to Mrs. Lewis, still unable to believe what I saw with my eyes. No one could fight mortic energy. And yet Mrs. Lewis breathed. Her heart beat. She was alive—and might now live long enough for her daughter to say goodbye.

I didn't understand. I'd never seen anything like this before. But I knew one thing for certain: what Camille had done was a miracle.

I smiled at Mrs. Lewis, but she evaded my eyes. And at the same time that I noticed the scent of lawn clippings and cologne had vanished, I realized Mrs. Lewis was crying.

2

B Y THE TIME I GOT HOME, it was well after midnight, and I expected the house to be silent. But when I pushed open the front door and heard the murmuring of voices coming from the kitchen, I knew that Big Ginny was awake and had someone with her.

At this hour, her having company could only mean one thing. Wearily, I walked into the kitchen to find my step-grandmother and a woman I didn't recognize sharing a cup of tea at the kitchen table. Spread in front of the woman was a collection of colored candles, a few saint figurines, and chicken bones smeared with blood.

At my entrance, Big Ginny's eyes lit up. "We was waiting for you," she said, a hint of admonishment rounding out her words. "You was supposed to be home almost half an hour ago."

"Sorry," I muttered. "I had some things to take care of after work."

Big Ginny frowned. "What things?"

I gave her a pointed look. "None of your business," I said. "What were you waiting on me for?"

I didn't really have to ask. If Big Ginny had a stranger in the house and there were chicken bones on the table, it meant she was doing a working. Big Ginny was a Conjure woman: a practitioner of African-American hoodoo. And whoever this woman was in our kitchen, she needed some kind of magic worked.

"Kezia, this is my friend, Nikki Jackson. Nikki, this is my granddaughter Kezia Bernard."

Nikki held out her hand, and I shook it, offering a smile. "Nice to meet you," I said.

The woman nodded, but didn't smile. "You, too."

I gave Nikki Jackson a once-over and determined that she was not, strictly speaking, Big Ginny's friend. Firstly, Big Ginny's only friends were the ladies from her gardening club, and they were all as old as Methuselah. Nikki Jackson was closer to my age, maybe early thirties. Secondly, Nikki Jackson looked like she was made of glass—if you spoke too loudly around her, she might shatter. Big Ginny didn't truck with those nervous types. She liked hardy people, folks you could call when shit went south. Nikki Jackson had none of the qualities my grandmother valued in other people.

Which meant Nikki Jackson was a paying customer. Well, good. Property taxes in Los Angeles were outrageous, and what I made working part-time at the hospice was barely enough to cover our bills. Still, I resented her being here. I was tired. I wanted a warm bed and sleep.

Big Ginny cleared her throat and beckoned for me to sit down, which I did, stifling a yawn. "Somebody been working roots on Nikki," Big Ginny explained. "Pretty sure we figured out who by now. Only one thing left to do."

I sighed and crossed my arms over my chest. "What kinda roots?" I asked.

Nikki dropped her eyes, pursing her lips together. Despite myself, my heart grew softer at this gesture. Black folks were often tight-lipped about personal matters. We were taught not to share our business with others from a young age. But I couldn't help Nikki if she didn't tell me what was up. My magic wasn't the mind-reading kind.

Big Ginny turned her gaze toward our guest. "Kezia can help us with this," she said, "but we got to tell her what's happening. I won't divulge information without your permission, so you got to give me permission."

The woman glanced between us, her expression nervous and perhaps a bit embarrassed. I waited patiently for her to decide. After a moment, she gave a small nod. Big Ginny took in a breath and turned to me. "She's been trying to have a baby, and she can't."

I blinked. "That's all?" I turned my attention to the woman. "Have you been to a doctor?"

The woman nodded. "There's nothing wrong with me. And I already have three healthy children. There is no reason on God's earth that I shouldn't be able to conceive. But I'm with a new man now, and I don't think my husband is happy about it," she explained. "And your grandmother here's been explaining to me that she thinks he's the one put this curse on me."

I rubbed my eyes and motioned toward the bones on the table. "Is that with the bones said? That it's the husband?"

Big Ginny huffed. "It's always the husband! Unless'n it's his side hussy. But this time, it's the husband. Take a look for yourself. What do you see?"

I shrugged. "Out of context, I don't see anything. I've never been as good at reading the bones as you. You say her husband put a curse on her, I believe you. What I don't know is what y'all want from me."

Big Ginny and Nikki exchanged looks. "Well," Nikki drawled, "my husband is dead."

I groaned, squeezing my eyes shut. I should have seen this coming. "So that's why y'all waited up for me. You need a necromancer."

Nikki dropped her eyes, and in my fatigue, I almost lost my patience. If all she needed was a necromancer, she didn't have to come here. She could have gone down to her local church or beauty salon. Our kind weren't common, but we weren't rare, either. There were enough of us to go around. Nature made sure of that; we had an important job to do. We were born with the ability to channel magic from our ancestors and speak to the dead. Born to heal a broken community. Among Black folks, going to see a necromancer was commonplace. So if Nikki came to me instead of her local necromancer, it meant she was worried about gossip. That softened my heart, but only a little. "But I can't give gifts, so don't ask."

"But you *can* speak to the dead?"

I nodded. "Yes."

Nikki leaned forward, her eyes full of pleading. "Your grandmother said you can find my husband on the other side. That you can convince him to let the curse go. Can you do that? Can you speak to my husband on the other side?"

I sighed, giving a rueful nod. "Yeah, probably. Curses from beyond the grave aren't common, but they're not as rare as you might think." I paused. "Your husband Black?"

Nikki blinked, gesturing toward her own skin. "What you think?" she asked.

I shrugged a shoulder. "Just cuz *you* Black don't mean *he* is." I rolled my eyes. "But anyway. When a person crosses over, they meet their ancestors. A lot of times, especially for our people, the ancestors teach them things. Magic being among those things." I licked my lips. "Where's your husband from?"

"New Orleans," she replied.

"Well, there you go," I said. "Probably didn't even have to look too far back to find somebody who would teach him how to work roots. People think the dead are angels. But in my experience, vindictive assholes in life remain vindictive assholes in death."

Nikki looked affronted. "He wasn't a vindictive asshole," she muttered.

I gestured toward her midsection. "He put a curse on you to prevent you from having a baby? Sounds vindictive to me."

Nikki chose not to argue, instead dropping her eyes to one side. "All right," she agreed. "Maybe he wasn't the man I like to pretend he was. So can you do it? Can you find him and ask him to break the curse?"

I dropped my head into my hands and gave Big Ginny a dour look. "You should have asked me first," I said. "I've had a long day."

Big Ginny huffed. "Not so long you can't help this woman have a baby."

I sighed. When Big Ginny got like this, there was nothing I could do to get her out of her mood. If I wanted to go to bed in peace, I was gonna have to comply.

I motioned towards Nikki. "Did you bring something of his? Something personal that I can use to find him on the other side?"

Without responding, Nikki opened a bag seated on the floor next to her. She pulled out a jewelry box and slid it across the table. I opened it to find it full of men's watches. "He collected those," Nikki said. "Wore one every day. Your grandmother said something close to the skin would be best. Will this work?"

I nodded. "I should be able to do something with this. I need to go make some preparations, though. It'll probably take me about 10 minutes. You good to wait?"

The woman nodded, relieved. "Yes, I can wait. I've got all night if you need it."

I grunted. "Better not take that long," I said as I rose from the table. I stopped halfway to the doorway. "It'll be $300," I said.

Big Ginny's eyes went wide at that number, but to her credit, she said nothing. We had a long-standing agreement that she could charge or not charge whatever she wanted for her Conjure work, but necromancy took a lot out of me. I didn't like doing it for other people. But if I was gonna do it, I was gonna get my damn coins.

The woman didn't even hesitate. "You got it," was all she said.

WHEN I RETURNED, I was dressed in a fresh night shift, my hair tucked carefully underneath a silk scarf. Necromancy often wore me out, and I would likely fall straight into bed after the ritual was over. Sometimes, my get-up turned people off. But I didn't care whether Nikki Jackson liked my outfit. We had work to do.

I sat down to the kitchen table and began arranging the accouterments I had brought from my bedroom on the table: essential oils, candles, incense, raven bones. When everything was arranged precisely how I wanted, I leaned forward onto my elbows, looking Nikki straight in the face. "Did my grandmother explain how this is gonna go down?"

Nikki nodded. "She said once you pass over to the other side, I'm not to talk to you or make any loud noises."

I nodded. "That's very important. If I get snatched back from the other side, it could be bad for both of us. And if that happens, I'm not going back. You feel me?"

Nikki's lips were trembling as she nodded. "I understand."

Satisfied, I prepared for the ritual. I turned off the kitchen lights and lit the candles. I had two: one for my female ancestors, the other from my male. I would need their guidance once I crossed over to help me find the gentleman in question. I took a small bottle of rose attar oil and anointed myself with drops on my wrists and temples. I did the same for Nikki and Big Ginny. "What's your husband's name?" I asked.

"Devon Jackson," she said.

It was a common enough name for our skinfolk, which made it easy to remember. The hardest part about this work was recalling the name of the deceased once I crossed over. It wasn't like anyone could remind me once I got there. I picked up each of the watches and slid them between my fingers, getting his energy all over my hands. I didn't like this part. Usually, when I handled objects from the deceased, my hands got numb or itchy. But tonight, nothing happened.

I lit the incense and closed my eyes, reciting a prayer from the book of Psalms. People think necromancers are wicked people who worship demons and Satan, but it's not true. Necromancers are only born to people in diaspora — people who were ripped away from their homeland, culture, and ancestors by slavery, trafficking, war, or other violence. Necromancy—the ability to speak to the dead—was nature's way of reconnecting lost tribes with their culture and heritage. It didn't have anything to do with the devil, and many of us who ended up in America, especially us Black folks, were Christians.

When my prayer ended, I opened my eyes and motioned for Nikki to give me her hands. She did, warily. I took them in my own. Her skin was warm, and her hands trembled in mine. Good. This kind of work was serious. Fear meant she took it seriously.

"I'm going to take some of your blood now," I said. "Are you ready?"

The woman nodded, and I retrieved a fresh lancet from the cupboard before returning to the table and quickly pricking the woman's finger. She winced but did not withdraw. I dribbled her blood onto the bones and when they were saturated enough, I released her fingers. I unwrapped a second lancet and pricked my own finger, drizzling my blood on top of Nikki's. Then, I smeared the blood over the bones until they were greasy with it.

I took the bones into my hands, prayed over them once more, then shook them before dropping them onto the table. All three of us leaned forward to peer at the bones, though only Big Ginny and I understood what they said. I recognized the message immediately: a powerful curse. An inability to conceive. A spiteful man. That was it, then. Big Ginny was right. And now, we were ready to get started.

I closed my eyes and pressed my hands together at my chest, my back ramrod straight. I took in deep, even, steadying breaths, letting my heartbeat slow and the tension ease out of my shoulders. My hands buzzed as the death current tuned in to my energy, availing itself to my beck and call. With my consciousness, I reached out to it, prodding it gently, acquainting myself with it. It responded quickly, used to my calling. The smells of death grew thicker in my nose. I felt a soft breeze on the backs of my hands as the death current quickened.

I breathed in, letting the current move through me. This was necessary to the work, but it was also dangerous. Necromancers had to reach out to death, but we also had to be prepared for death to reach back. Opening ourselves to the death current meant that we risked an accelerated timeline of our own. Mess around and absorb the energy instead of letting it pass through you, and you might find yourself crossing over to the other side without a way to get back.

Death was very welcoming that way. It accepted all comers.

It didn't take long for the transformation to begin, sinking me deeper into my trance. In a moment, I heard the familiar sounds: the beating of drums, ululations of women, the shouts of men, whispered prayers, the crackling of fire, and the shrieks of children. Every necromancer experiences crossing the veil, the thin membrane that separates the world of the living from the world of the dead, differently. But for me, crossing over was always accompanied by the sounds of my ancestors, of Africa, of family.

For me, crossing the veil felt like coming home.

As I crossed over, I was no longer conscious of my physical body. My awareness transferred to the other side, the place where the dead congregated. I opened my astral eyes and looked around. As usual, I had landed on a nondescript shore-line, surrounded by the spirits of the deceased. The faces were all Black: Africans and people descended from Africans. They looked on me with more curiosity than suspicion, but none of them spoke.

"I'm looking for Devon Jackson," I said.

The assembled spirits exchanged looks, grumbling amongst themselves. Sometimes, the dead didn't like to speak to strangers. I held up my astral hands, apologetic. "I'm here on behalf of his wife. Her name is Nikki Jackson. She's looking for him. Is he here?"

It was a man who spoke. Judging by his dress, he probably died recently. "He's one of our kinfolk," the man said, only a hint of hesitation in his voice. "But he's not here."

I balked at that. "Not here? How do you mean?"

A woman spoke up this time, her apparel suggesting that she was perhaps not American. Something about the choice of cloth and how it cut across her body intimated that she was from the islands, perhaps having lived generations ago. "Devon Jackson? You sure?"

I nodded, my brow creased. "I'm sure. You *are* his kinfolk, right?"

The woman nodded. "That's right. Just *make no sense* you come looking for him here."

Again, I didn't understand. "Why?"

The woman frowned. "Cuz he ain't dead."

Stunned, my mouth dropped open, but no sound came out. I frowned, shaking my head. "He's not dead? But his wife—"

A general chuckle rippled throughout the assembled spirits. "He's tricky," another girl said. "He been praying to us a lot more often lately. I think he been learning hoodoo from his grandpops." She nodded towards the man who had greeted me. "Tell her, Percy. You been teaching him, yeah?"

Percy scowled, his lips pursed, but he didn't deny it. The girl laughed. "Well, he ain't gonna admit it, cuz you ain't family, and Percy like to keep his shit locked up *tight*. But I'll tell you, one sister to another. He ain't dead. He just ain't wanna be with that woman no more."

I had more questions, but I could already tell the interview was over. The assembled spirits began to dissipate, leaving me alone on the shore. I could stay and try to get more answers, but I wasn't being paid for answers. I didn't like to linger on the other side. Didn't seem healthy.

I offered silent thanks to the spirits before allowing the death current to take me home. When I regained consciousness back in Big Ginny's kitchen, I blinked a few times, clapping my hands in front of my face and speaking my name out loud to ground myself. To make sure that my spirit remained anchored in my body. When I was sure I was back, I let out my breath in a whoosh.

"I have good news and bad news," I said. "The good news is the curse will be easier to break than we thought." I glanced between Big Ginny and Nikki and forced myself to smile, but neither woman returned my expression. Fair enough. "The bad news is, the reason it will be easier to break is because Devon Jackson isn't dead."

For a slow, stretched out moment, no one made a sound. All I could hear was a clock ticking in the next room. Eventually, Big Ginny gave a low whistle, folding her hands in her lap and shaking her head as she clucked her teeth. But Nikki merely stared at me wide-eyed before anger settled over the contours of her face. I knew this was coming, but I was still surprised when she blurted out, "You don't know what the fuck you're talking about!"

"You actually *see* his body?" I snapped.

Nikki brushed a stray lock of hair behind an ear, clearing her throat and giving her head a little shake. "Well, no. By the time he died, we'd been separated almost two years. I hadn't seen him, but he was supposed to be staying with his people out in Georgia. His family and I weren't on good terms. I wasn't invited to the funeral." Slowly, her body began to shake. "But this can't be right. It *can't*. What kind of people could lie about a man's death?" Her voice rose sharply, her fingers curling into her palm. "Lying to me is one thing, but we have *children*! How can he still be alive? How can..." Her words trailed off as she leaned her head back, blinking back fresh tears. I saw her nails bite deeper into her palm. Any deeper and the skin would break. "There just has to be a mistake. *Has* to be."

I shrugged. "I don't know shit about shit, and I don't know nothing about you or your family. But I do know how to speak to the ancestors. I talked to his family. They said he's still alive and he ran out on you." I saw Big Ginny wince at the way I phrased that. I should have been more delicate, but it was late, and I was tired. "When I touched his watches, I didn't feel anything. That should have tipped me off, but you just never know. This explains it. He's still alive."

Nikki hesitated before asking, "How does his being alive make it easier to break the curse?"

"The most effective way to undo root work isn't to break it," Big Ginny explained. "The best way is to turn it back on whoever put words on you. When they feel their own bad juju come back on them, they stop tryna do more harm. Breaking a curse just pisses em off; they're like to try again. Turning it back on them makes em more like to stop. But you can't turn no curse on a dead man. You can only turn a curse on the living."

I watched as Nikki's anger was replaced by disbelief and then finally gave way to anguish. Her face crumpled, shoulders trembling as she mewled. With my job complete, I pushed myself away from the table and stood. I gestured toward the accessories I had brought from my bedroom. "I'mma leave these here," I said to Big Ginny. "I'm tired. I'm going to bed." I turned one last time to Nikki. "I'm sorry to be the one to break this news to you. Please leave the money on the table before you go."

If she made any objection, I didn't hear it as I closed my bedroom door behind me and fell into bed.

3

I ARRIVED EARLY TO MY SHIFT the next evening. The scheduling coordinator had me working odd shifts to keep me from spending too much time around my coworkers. Being a necromancer had a lot of upside: we could speak to the dead, access the magic of our ancestors, and channel it to individuals, offering them all kinds of fantastic magical benefits. And the more we gave magic to others, the more our own magic grew.

But it also carried a hefty price.

All of us had an affliction, a condition that caused other people to wither away and die the more time they spent in our presence. Most people were immune, but it was impossible to predict who was susceptible until they started getting sick. Even then, it was hard to tell. The early symptoms of necromantic exposure sickness (or *the blues* as it was colloquially called) were nearly identical to run-of-the-mill depression (hence the nickname). So while it was unlikely that my coworkers would die from being around me, nobody was willing to take that risk.

Which, you know. I couldn't blame them.

So I worked short shifts, only a few hours of which over-lapped with any of my coworkers at the same time. It kept them safe, but it meant I didn't get to know them well. It meant I didn't really have any friends. So when I walked into the nurse's station and saw Jennifer, Camille, and Michael all smiling in my direction, my heart skipped a beat. I shrugged out of my jacket and hung it up. "Hey guys. What's going on?"

Jennifer gave me a little finger wave as she took a bite of her sandwich. Jennifer was a certified nurse's assistant like me, and the only other Black staffer. She was friendly but a little on the silly side. "What up, Kezia! How's it going? You got that Godsend yet? I need a *gift*."

I sank down into one of the empty chairs, dramatically rolling my eyes. "Are you for real gonna ask me this every day for the rest of my life until I die? No Godsend; no gifts to give." I removed my watch and jewelry and tucked them into my purse. "Are you just asking to fuck with me, or do you really want one? Cuz if you really want a gift, I know a necro-mancer not too far from here. Runs a magic shop called Necro Sis. Her name's Opal."

Michael glanced up from his magazine. "What's a Godsend? *I* want one."

Jennifer sniffed. "Well, you can't have one. They're a Black thing."

I bristled. "That's...not exactly true," I grumbled. I turned to Michael, whose brow was cocked like this information actu-ally interested him. "A Godsend is a necromancer's ability to channel magic from our ancestors to an individual. People call that magic a *gift*. It usually only lasts for a few weeks, but it gives the receiver special abilities: mind reading, healing, seeing the future, stuff like that." I shrugged. "But I don't have the Godsend, so I can't give any gifts."

Jennifer sighed dramatically, leaning back in her chair. "Kezia's a necromancer who can't actually *do* necromancer stuff."

She wasn't trying to get my hackles up, but she succeeded anyway. "I can do *plenty* of 'necromancer stuff'," I said, trying to keep my voice level. "I just can't do *that* particular thing."

Michael side-eyed me. "So if *you* can't even do it, and you're Black...why did Jennifer say it was a Black thing?"

"Because in this country, most necromancers *are* Black. And we can only grant gifts to others in our own community. Which is fair," I said, with a grin. "Y'all got that white privilege. We get magic." That earned me both chuckles and groans. "But I can't even do *that* because I don't have the Godsend to begin with."

Michael hrmmed. "Lame. So why don't you have it?"

That's personal, I thought with bitterness. But getting frigid with somebody who wanted to understand me wasn't the best way to win friends and influence people. So instead, I wrinkled my nose and said, "Well, it's complicated. But the short answer is that to receive your Godsend, you have to first contact your nearest departed ancestor. In my case, that's my mom. She died giving birth to me. But for some reason—and I don't know why—I haven't been able to find her on the other side. So I can't access the magic of my ancestors. No Godsend for me."

Michael looked back down at this magazine, interest suddenly gone. "Sucks."

"Yeah," I agreed, trying to keep the pain from my voice. My lack of Godsend was a topic I was sensitive about. "Anyway, where's Frankie? I thought he was on the schedule for tonight."

The others shared a look I couldn't read. "You didn't hear?" Jennifer said around a bite of tuna sandwich. "I thought everybody heard about this. Kezia, you've really got to get on the group chat. You miss out on all the good gossip." She leaned forward, pushing her sandwich to one side. "Frankie got canned. They caught him putting cameras in some of the patients' rooms. Can you imagine? How freaky do you have to be to want to spy on old people?"

I frowned. "Frankie was spying on people? That doesn't seem right."

Camille made a show of examining her nails. "It's *not* right," she said. "That's the point. That's why they fired him."

"That's obviously not what I meant," I said, sucking my teeth. "I mean that doesn't sound like Frankie. He just never struck me as the voyeur type."

Michael closed his magazine and pinched the bridge of his nose. "Seriously, Kezia, that's not something you can tell from spending two hours a week with someone."

Jennifer glanced at the clock. "Okie, break time's over. I'm gonna go check on Mrs. Larson. Oh, Kezia? Can you do a round of room checks with a broom? Some of the patients have been complaining about bugs. Margaret called an exterminator."

Again, Michael cocked an eyebrow. "Could that be because *someone* keeps dropping her granola bar crumbs all over the place?"

Jennifer looked offended; her chin even wobbled a bit. "I never eat in the patients' rooms." She turned her attention back to me. "Also, your aunt was asking for you earlier."

Aunt Fat was Big Ginny's older cousin and had been at the

hospice for longer than I had been working there, which meant she'd been there almost five months. Her insurance probably wouldn't allow her to stay much past six months, so I didn't know what to hope for. On the one hand, she was Big Ginny's only surviving relative, if you didn't count me and my brother. For that reason, I wanted her to live longer. But on the other hand, I knew Aunt Fat was suffering. And we sure couldn't pay her expenses if her insurance ran out. It was a dilemma, and not one I endured alone.

Our healthcare system left a lot to be desired.

I brushed my curls for my forehead. "Ok, thanks for letting me know. I'll go check in on her."

"Do you want me to come with you?" Camille was standing now, brushing imaginary wrinkles from her perfectly pressed scrubs. "I have time. Do you want me to? Come?"

I frowned. "What for? She's *my* aunt."

Camille returned my frown. "Yes, but she's *our* patient. I thought she might need more pain meds."

"What happened last night with Mrs. Lewis?" I asked suddenly. I didn't know I was going to bring it up until the words were out of my mouth. "She was ready to go. But some-how, you...*talked* her out of it. How did you do that?"

Camille made a dismissive motion with her hand as though implying that my question lacked importance. "I guess you could say I have a gift." She said this in the same way some people announce their astrological sign—half fact, half mystery. "Not all of her children were there, and her family wasn't ready for her to go. I hate watching them suffer, espe-cially when I can do something about it. So I just...convinced her to stay a while longer."

I sucked in a breath. "I've never seen anything like that before."

Camille shrugged a slim shoulder. If she noted the awe in my voice, she didn't let on. "I guess not a lot of people can do it, but I've always been this way. My mother said I was very persuasive as a child." She grinned, chuckling at a private memory. "I pretty much always got my way, just because I could talk anyone into seeing things from my perspective. I don't know," she concluded. "It's just a gift of persuasion."

I nodded. "That's some gift. In fact…"

Camille's brows lifted. "What?"

I grinned. "If I didn't know better, I'd say you've been getting gifts from necromancers. But those gifts are temporary, and you're…well, I don't think you're part of any community in diaspora. You're not Jewish, are you?"

Camille laughed, shaking her head. "No, I haven't been getting gifts from necromancers. Come on, Kezia. Even us non-magic folks get cool natural talents *sometimes*." She gave me a mocking look of admonishment, wagging a finger as she disappeared down the corridor and around a corner.

I turned back to my remaining colleagues. "All right. I'm gonna go check on my aunt. Michael, you're off, right?" I asked, checking the clock.

He folded his arms across his chest. "Was supposed to be, but with Frankie not on the schedule, I'm picking up a shift. I'll be here a couple more hours, though I'll be mostly hiding out in the break room. They can make me stay, but they can't make me play. Plus, no offense, Kezia, but I'm not tryna catch the blues from you." He smiled and shooed me away.

Fair enough.

Aunt Fat's room was at the end of a hallway with a faulty florescent light. As I walked down the hallway, the soles of my rubber clogs silent on the linoleum and the light flickering overhead, I felt like I was inside a bad horror movie. No matter how many times I walked these halls, I still wasn't used to how heavily the smell of death clung to every corner of the building.

I entered my aunt's room without announcing myself. When she saw me, she smiled and patted her bedside. I came and sat next to her, giving her a soft kiss on the cheek.

"How you doing, auntie?" I asked.

Aunt Fat clucked her tongue against the roof of her mouth and chuckled, a rattling sound in her chest. *It won't be long*, I thought. I needed to get Big Ginny down here to say her final farewells. But I pushed that thought out of my mind as something to worry about tomorrow.

"I'm bored out of my mind," she said, her speech slow and labored. "Ain't you got none of them romance novels you can bring me? One of those good kinds that don't hold back on all the details."

I laughed and shook my head. "You can't even hold a book! The hell you finna do with a romance novel?"

Aunt Fat rolled her eyes. "I ain't no dummy. They got them romance novels you can listen to. What you call it? An audiobook? Yeah, an audiobook. Girl, you best *bring me* a audiobook. I might be too old to read but I still got needs."

I faked a gagging sound even as I laughed. "Auntie! You better stop. I don't need to hear that." When my chuckles subsided, I gave her another smile. "I'll see what I can do. Any other requests? Jennifer said you were asking for me."

Aunt Fat was silent a moment, her gaze listing sideways. After a while, she lifted her eyes to meet mine, her eyes locking with mine. "Baby girl," she said, "I need a favor. I don't know if you're gonna like it."

I already didn't like it, but I didn't let on. I squeezed my aunt's fingers. "What is it?"

She swallowed. "You know how they say you have a psychic bond with anyone you've…been *intimate* with?"

My brows drew together in worry. "I've heard that," I drawled.

Aunt Fat sucked in a noisy breath. "Well, I ain't never believed it before, but I do now." She turned away from me, unable to meet my eyes. "Someone I knew a long time ago—in a biblical way—well, he's been haunting me."

My frown deepened. "Haunting you how?"

My aunt continued to look the other direction. "He won't let me die," she whispered. "He comes at night. I been so close to death several times now, Kezia. So close I could feel the Lord calling me home. But when I try to go into the light, my old lover appears, and I can't cross over. He's keeping me here, keeping me sick so I can't go home to the Lord." She was crying now, her voice shaking with emotion. "I *been* ready to go, Kee. I can tell I ain't supposed to be here no more. I can't feel the sunlight that comes through the windows. I don't taste the food they bring me to eat. Even my breathing don't feel natural—it's just my chest going up and down but ain't no urgency to it. My body's just going through the motions. I ain't supposed to *be* here no more, and I know it, my body know it, the world know it. But Jinabbott keep showing up, trapping me here in this broken body."

I surmised from the fact that she wanted *my* help that Jinabbott was dead. I tightened my grip on my aunt's fingers. "Why would he do that? Why would he keep you from dying?"

She drew in a wet, crackling breath. "To keep me from seeing our baby girl in Heaven. So he can have her all to himself."

For a moment, I couldn't speak. My throat closed up and

RITES OF PASSAGE | 31

ran dry. Sometimes, the old people got confused. As a death worker, I knew that. But it was different now that it was happening to someone I loved. Different now that it was happening to my aunt. "Auntie? Are you okay? You don't..." My voice broke, sudden tears blurring my vision. "You don't have a daughter."

Now, Aunt Fat turned her head to face me, her eyes finding mine in the dimness. "You don't know everything," she whispered. "Please, Kezia. I can't stay in this body forever. I'm ready to go. Please stop Jinabbott. Do whatever magic you got to do, but please make him let me go. I'm begging you."

A knock on the door interrupted our moment. Camille poked her head in, a little frown playing over her lips. "Kezia? I'm sorry to interrupt. Margaret's looking for you."

I sighed and kissed my aunt. "We can talk about this later," I promised. Aunt Fat made no indication that she heard.

I followed Camille to the nurse's station where my boss, Margaret, was scolding Jennifer, a granola bar clutched in her hand.

"Low blood sugar is not an excuse," Margaret was saying. "You should've had dinner before you got here."

Jennifer looked like she was about to burst into tears. "I did, but I'm *hungry*," she whined, lowering the offending granola bar into her lap. "I have a high metabolism, Margaret. I can't help it. And you don't want me to faint again, do you?"

"What do you mean *again*?"

Michael looked up from his reading material long enough to say, "She passed out last week tending to Mr. Bennett. She posted it on the group chat."

"I woke up *on the floor*," Jennifer whined. "I think it really scared Mr. Bennett. He *looked* scared, anyway."

"Well, fine, but you need to find a better solution,"

Margaret continued. "You don't see anybody else stuffing their face at all hours of the night. Look at Camille. She's already been here for hours and she hasn't even taken a meal break."

At this, Camille flipped her hair over her shoulder. "Actually, I'm hungry, too."

Jennifer thumbed over her shoulder toward the break room. "I've got more granola bars in the back," she offered. "You want me to get you one? They're the honey kind."

Margaret gaped, incredulous. "Really? Jennifer, I *just* gave you a warning for this! We've got bugs!"

"It's just crickets," Jennifer mumbled, ducking her head low. "Everybody gets crickets."

But Camille only shook her head, focusing on something in the distance. "I'm allergic to honey," she said absently. "Thanks, but I don't think granola bars are gonna do it. I probably need green vegetables or something. I'm not feeling so great."

"You don't *look* so great," Jennifer agreed. When Margaret threw her another incredulous look, Jennifer cringed. "What? I'm just saying she looks kind of pale."

Camille grimaced, but she didn't look offended. "Yeah. I just got a phone call. Diablo died."

Jennifer frowned, searching her memory for a patient named Diablo. "Who?"

"Diablo. My dog."

My brows rose in surprise. "You have a dog?"

Camille shrugged. "Not anymore."

The energy in the room plummeted, and I suddenly felt like an asshole. It was a stupid thing to say, and I hadn't meant anything by it. I just didn't see Camille as a dog person.

But what did I know?

"Actually, I think I'm going to take a smoke break." Camille lifted her gaze to Margaret. "That okay?"

Margaret shooed her off, and Camille slipped down the hall, out the front door.

"Kezia, you are smooth as silk," Michael said, not even bothering to look up from his magazine. "Honestly, your bedside manner is—" He kissed his fingers in a chef's kiss. I felt even more of an ass.

I knew Margaret wanted to speak to me about something, but I wasn't going to feel right until I apologized to Camille. "Let me go talk to her," I said. Margaret nodded, and I turned on my heel, following Camille into the night.

I found her sitting on a bench just outside the parking lot, smoking one of her extra-long cigarettes. Nobody smoked anymore, but Camille somehow made it look posh. She looked like a model from a vintage Pall Mall advertisement.

I shuffled over to her, hands dug deep into my pockets. "I'm sorry," I said. "I didn't mean to be insensitive."

Camille blew out a thin ring of silvery smoke and gave a shrug, the neckline of her v-necked scrubs traveling slightly down a shoulder. She'd lost weight recently; I hadn't noticed until now. Her shoulder was lightly freckled with a dark smear of something that in the moonlight looked like flaking shoe polish. When Camille caught me looking, she adjusted herself, tugging her collar gently into place. "It's fine," she said. "It's kind of weird, right? We work in hospice helping people die all the time. But when it gets close to you…" She shrugged. "I had Diablo for ten years. I was pretty attached. I knew he was close last night. I tried to talk him back from death the way I do the patients, but I guess he couldn't understand a word I said, so he died anyway."

Camille blew out another lungful of smoke, and the scent

filled my nostrils. It didn't quite cover up the fragrance of her perfume, a heady rose oud too mature and heavy for her. The combination of fragrances made my stomach churn. "Well, dogs can't live forever," I said, meaning the words to be comforting. But spoken aloud, they sounded hollow. I tried again. "I mean, even if he understood you. Maybe he even *wanted* to stay with you. But that's not how biology works. Cells can't regenerate forever. Still, I'm sorry for your loss," I added when I realized nothing else I could say would matter at all. Death is always hard for those left behind.

Camille took a long drag off her cigarette. "I have a lot of empathy, you know? When the patients are dying, I feel them out and discern what they really want. If I feel like they really want to die and they're ready to go, then I facilitate that. Just like you do. But if I sense that they want to hold on, that they're waiting for someone or something..." Again, that shrug. "There's no formula to it or anything. It's just a knack I have. Same way some people are funny or have perfect pitch. I can talk people back from death." She smiled as she said this, flashing even, white teeth. But there was no joy in it. She looked deeply sad.

"That's a real gift," I said.

Camile nodded. "I know."

"Is that why you got into hospice care?" I asked. "Because you can talk people back from death?"

Camille barked a bitter laugh, tossing her hair off her shoulder as she gazed skyward. "No. I started out as a labor and delivery nurse. But I pissed off the wrong doctor one night and was relieved of my duties. Like I said," she said, a note of bitterness entering her voice, "I have a lot of empathy. Some of these women giving birth? They don't even know what their options are. The doctors remove all agency from them. I wanted to remind them they could refuse treatment and ask for the birth they want. Turns out, doctors don't like having their authority fucked with."

We were silent for a while, Camille smoking her cigarette, and I gazing up at the stars. There weren't many; too much ambient light in Los Angeles to see much of the Milky Way. But I always looked for the stars every chance I got.

"How about you?" she asked. "What are you doing in this job?"

I was ready for this question, yet I still took my time answering. I cleared my throat and fidgeted with a stray curl. "I studied biology in college," I said. "But one of my professors suggested I might be better off in thanatology—using my passion for life to help the dying. So here I am."

Camille nodded without meeting my eyes. "Well, I guess it's safer for you here. I mean if one of our patients gets the blues—well, at least they were gonna die anyway, right?"

I cringed. I didn't like hearing it put that way, even if it was true. "Yeah. Something like that."

Camille hrmmed, the corners of her mouth tugging into a frown. "That sucks. Your affliction, I mean. Magic seems like it would be a cool thing to have, but that's a shitty trade to make for it."

I couldn't have said it better myself.

4

W HEN MY SHIFT WAS OVER, I made my way back to Aunt Fat's room. She was awake when I arrived, but she didn't greet me. I tiptoed to her bedside where I settled into a chair. I waited for a while, hoping she would say something. When it became clear she wouldn't, I cleared my throat. "Aunt Fat? I need you to think about this. Do you really have a daughter?"

Aunt Fat didn't respond, and I frowned, leaning forward. Maybe she hadn't heard. But then a sharp intake of breath followed by sniffling let me know that she was crying. "Her name's Charmaine," she said.

"Charmaine," I repeated. A shiver went down my spine, and my skin pimpled over. Somehow, I knew this was all real. Aunt Fat was lucid and clear, she was being haunted by an old lover, and she had a daughter I'd never heard of named Charmaine. Strung together like that, the thoughts were dizzying and put me off balance. I thought I *knew* my aunt.

But maybe you don't ever *really* know another person.

"All right," I said. "I'm gonna help you. We can do this now, if you're ready."

Now, my aunt turned her face to me, her eyes shining with tears. "You don't have your tools," she said.

I shook my head. "I don't think I need them. They help me focus, especially when I'm working with people I'm not related to. But I don't absolutely need them."

Now, Aunt Fat tried on a smile. "You ain't really related to me," she said.

I clucked my tongue. It was true that we weren't blood kin; she was Big Ginny's cousin, but Big Ginny was my father's stepmother. But Big Ginny raised me; as far as I was concerned, that meant more than blood. "The hell you say. You're one quarter of all the family I got left in this world. Now. What's this man's name?"

Aunt Fat bit down on her lip before answering. "Jinabbott Watson."

I took her hands into my own and silently began the ritual. With my consciousness, I reached out towards the death current, pulling it gently toward me so I could ride on its back through the veil where I sought the man Aunt Fat was so afraid of. I repeated his name over and over in my mind: Jinabbott Watson. Jinabbott Watson. Jinabbott Watson.

Every time I rode through the veil was a little different; tonight, however, was *very* different. Usually when I crossed over, I landed on a nondescript shoreline, pale sand against a colorless sky. The person I was looking for, or sometimes their ancestors or kin, would be waiting for me—sometimes happily, other times not. Usually, I'd be greeted by music and laughter, the muted sounds of conversation.

But this was nothing like that.

I was standing on a rotting wood porch, thick, humid air

heavy around me. I saw murky water, gnarled trees growing from the muck, ropes of moss dripping from the branches to meet the knobbed cypress knees that jutted from beneath. I smelled mud, sulfur, decaying vegetation. In the distance, I heard the call of birds.

I had never been here before, not in real life and not in my visits to the other side, but I recognized the landscape from Big Ginny's stories. I was in the Louisiana bayou where Aunt Fat and Big Ginny grew up.

Across from me, on the other side of the porch, a man sat in a rocking chair, a thin blanket draped over his knees despite the heat, a pair of knitting needles in his hands. He was old, with a neat, snow-white afro darkening to gray at the temples. His skin was a few shades darker than mine, a rich umber with cool undertones. He didn't look up when I arrived, his attention on the knitting project in his hands. Though his fingers were gnarled and arthritic, bulging, painful-looking knuckles that glistened with sweat, his knitting was smooth and efficient. White yarn danced over the needles, each stitch adding form to whatever he was creating.

Truthfully, I'd never seen a man knit before. Despite myself, I was charmed.

"Are you Mr. Jinabbott Watson?" I asked.

The man turned rheumy eyes in my direction, a sneer on his face. "It's *John Albert*," he corrected. "Who's asking?"

Under different circumstances, I might have chuckled. Of course his name was John Albert. I tutted at Aunt Fat's aggressively country pronunciation. "My name's Kezia Bernard. I'm Fatima Jamerson's niece," I said, using Aunt Fat's maiden name.

If my revelation surprised him, he didn't let on. Instead, he pulled the blanket on his lap up just a little higher. "Now that's a name I ain't heard in a long time," he said. "In my day, folks called her Fat. What she want?"

This was the tricky part. If this man was working roots on my aunt, I needed to convince him to stop. But usually, convincing required a bit of accusation. And this man was already prickly. I had to proceed with caution.

"She's very ill," I said. "I've been caring for her for the past several months, and it's time for her to go. She's ready to die and reunite with her family and ancestors. But, the way she tells it, you're not letting her pass on."

He barely looked up from his knitting, the only sound the clink of his needles against each other. I could almost feel the rhythm of his knitting: *knit one, purl two. Knit one, purl two.* He leaned back into his chair, dark eyes narrowing as he gazed back at me. "You don't know what the hell you're talking about," he said.

It was the second time in as many days that someone had accused me of that, and it was getting on my nerves. "No, sir, I'm sure I don't know the whole story. I'm just here as Fatima's envoy. She wants to die. And I'm here to ask you to let her."

"I don't know you," he snarled. Then, with a nimbleness I couldn't have predicted, John Albert leaped from his rocking chair, the blanket thrown from his lap. As the cloth fluttered to the ground and the knitting needles clattered on the wood flooring, a cloud of moths rose from the floorboards, soaring into the sky and flapping at my face, their wings beating fretfully until I stumbled backward, screeching.

I hit the floor hard, and when I landed, I couldn't move. All around me, the bayou grew thick with the sounds of life, the noise of insects and wildlife impossibly loud in my ears. The buzz of mosquitos competed with the screams of cicadas and the deep, echoing call of bullfrogs. Even the hissing of snakes and the beating of bird's wings shrilled high, blotting out my ability to think. Paralyzed with fear, I lay on the porch floor, my eyes wide as the noise of the swamp threatened to drive me insane.

Finally, I found mobility. I clawed my way along the floor, my liquid knees refusing to let me stand. John Albert inched toward me, in no hurry, a twisted grin across his face as he held out his hand, almost as though to help me rise. But the darkness that clouded his features warned me otherwise. He wasn't trying to help.

Then, out of nowhere, came the snakes.

They slithered up the porch steps, their tongues darting in and out, smelling the air, looking for me. My heart hammered against my ribs, threatening to explode from my chest. My skin was slick with sweat; my mouth tasted of copper and bile. I scuttled along the wooden planks, trying to outrun the snakes, but they were so fast.

Scaly skin touched mine. Cool, dry. Electricity danced between us.

That's when I screamed.

A bolt of energy hit me square in my chest, knocking me out of the other side and back into my physical body. I gasped, shaking and sweating as I regained consciousness. When I'd first crossed over, I'd been sitting in a chair next to my aunt's bed. Now, I was on the floor, on the other side of the room. I looked to my aunt, whose cheeks were tear stained.

I was hyperventilating, my entire body shaking. What had I just seen? Nothing, and I mean *nothing* like that had ever happened before. What the hell had John Albert done? And what the hell was up with the insects, the frogs, the *snakes?* No, sir, snakes were a whole new level of absolutely not. I'd never had such an awful experience on the other side.

Never.

"Baby?"

I looked to my aunt, but I couldn't speak. I suddenly felt ravaged, a bone-deep fatigue gnawing at my insides. I had to fight just to keep my eyes open. I tried to work my mouth, to tell my aunt what I'd seen, but I didn't need to. The look on her face told me she already knew.

"He won't let me go, will he?" she asked.

I trembled, fingers fluttering at the base of my throat, trying to help my words find purchase. "I'm so sorry," I breathed at last.

We sat together in silence for a long time until Aunt Fat fell asleep. I prayed, wracked with guilt, that she wouldn't wake.

And yet, somehow, I was filled with a cold dread and the certainty that she would.

I SLEPT in the next day. By the time I finally dragged myself out of my bedroom and headed toward the kitchen and the smell of coffee, it was already half past noon. Big Ginny was sitting at the kitchen table, a cup of coffee in one hand and a book in the other. When she saw me, she placed the book face down on the table and gestured toward the coffeemaker.

"I just put on a fresh pot," she said. "Had a feeling you'd be up soon. You sleep okay?"

I shuffled over to the coffeemaker and poured myself a cup of black coffee before joining my grandmother at the table. "I slept fine. Look. I got to tell you something, but I don't want you to get mad."

Big Ginny grunted. "Well, I can't promise nothing till I

know what you finna say. I might get mad anyway, and then I've already broken my promise."

"No, that's not what I mean." I took a sip of the coffee. It had already grown cool. "I mean I'm about to break someone's confidence and I don't want you to be mad at me. But I think you might be the only person who can help me, so I'm telling you."

Big Ginny raised an eyebrow. "Okay. What is it?" Big Ginny was too eager, and I had to bite back a smile. She had a lot of high points, but she was also an insufferable gossip.

"Did you know Aunt Fat had a daughter?"

Instantly, my grandmother's face turned to stone. She looked away, but not fast enough. "No, she ain't," she said.

"Yes, she did," I said leaning forward. "She told me as much last night. But it looks like you already knew that, didn't you?"

Big Ginny blew out her cheeks in a frustrated sigh, running her fingers over her hair. "You know that ain't the kind of stuff we talk about in this household," she said, her voice ringed with steel. "Why did she tell you that?"

I drummed my fingers on the table. "She says her daughter's father has been haunting her. She's…well, she's *terrified* of him. She says she's ready to die, but he appears in her room and holds her back. She asked for my help. Presumably to bind him so he can't mess with her anymore."

Big Ginny's frown deepened. "That all she say?"

I clucked my tongue. "Ain't that enough?"

Big Ginny's nostrils flared. "Lord have mercy, if she wasn't my dying cousin, I'd kill her."

I blinked, settling back into my chair, surprise pulling my brows toward my hairline. "Why? What are you not telling me?"

Big Ginny grumbled, licking her lips and worrying her thumbs over her knuckles. Then her focus went soft like she was conjuring up a memory, and she plopped her chin into her hands. "When I was growing up, magic was part of our everyday lives. My mama was a Conjure woman like her mama before her. I grew up mixing remedies for young men with heart sickness, old women with bad hips, and siblings involved in drawn-out family squabbles. But we wasn't the only workers in town. Back then, there was a lot of us. Well, maybe not a lot, but enough to go around. Most folks specialized. Our neighborhood had a Conjure doctor who specialized in settling domestic disputes, and a root worker who specialized in potions for the body. But all of us worked the same kind of magic, you know. It was all hoodoo spiritualism. Except for one man."

Big Ginny pushed away from the table and went to the cupboard, fetching herself a cigar. She pulled a cigar cutter from the silverware drawer and snipped off the end. "Some say he got his powers from the devil. Some say he was a changeling—not human at all, but a wicked fairy got switched with a human child. In any case, he was different. Dark, beautiful skin and a deep, throaty voice. Everybody loved looking at him. Didn't nobody want to get too near to him, though."

She fished a wooden matchstick from a pocket and lit it on the stove. Then she lit the cigar, pulling deeply with a look of reverie on her face. I hadn't seen Big Ginny smoke a cigar in a long time. It must have been the story igniting memories that did it.

"He was what we called an animage—a wild worker. He worked animal possession and drew his magic from their spirits. That kind of wild magic was frowned upon, because animals don't have morals. And his magic didn't, either. His magic was wild, vicious, and raw—all about survival. He would work roots on anybody did him wrong, and I heard more than a few stories about somebody who ended up in they grave on account of messing with him. You didn't mess with animage John Albert. Everybody knew that."

The cigar smoke was growing too thick for my liking. I got up and opened a window. "So how did Aunt Fat get involved with him?"

Big Ginny clucked her tongue against the roof of her mouth. "Well, he'd had his eye on Fat for a long time. She always had a lot of suitors. Drove her daddy crazy," she said with a phlegmy chuckle. "Normally, John Albert wouldn't have stood a chance. But one Christmas, a boy from church gave Fat a parakeet as a gift. Boy, Fat *loved* that bird. Oh, she fawned over it. Treated it like a person. And after she'd had the bird for a while, ole John Albert shows up, asking to court Fat.

"Of course, her daddy said no but Fat was ornery, and for reasons nobody understood at the time, she agreed to go out with him. And eventually, she fell in love with him. Even got herself in a bad way."

I knew enough about old-people euphemisms to know that getting in a bad way meant Fat got knocked up. "It was the bird, wasn't it? He possessed the bird and used it to weave a love spell on her. The more she loved the bird, the more she loved him."

Big Ginny nodded. "That's right. He was *good*. He could possess multiple creatures at a time. And while he was working love magic on Fat with that bird, he could also be out possessing owls and crickets and doing who-knows-what-else. The problem was, the human soul wasn't meant to be parceled out like that. When you throw your soul, you supposed to throw the whole thing. But he threw his soul into too many pieces at once and it started to affect him. Made him a little mad." She circled her forefinger around her temple. "He got real possessive of Fat, and even more possessive of the child she was growing in her womb."

I nodded. "Okay. So Aunt Fat was pregnant with the animage's baby. Then what?"

Big Ginny shrugged. "Then nothing. After the baby was born, the spell broke. Fat realized what had happened. She was scared of her own baby—wouldn't hold her, wouldn't nurse her. Then one night, Fat disappeared. Up and run off. Alone." She cleared her throat. "We heard many years later that the little girl didn't make it. Scarlet fever."

I whistled low and blew over the surface of my coffee. "I never knew any of that."

Big Ginny made a regretful sound in the back of her throat. "Fat regretted leaving that baby behind her whole life. She did what she thought she had to do," she amended quickly, "but you know how it is. Regret stays with you. At least once she passes, she can make amends. But." She gave a lame shrug and took a long pull from her cigar, holding the smoke in her mouth before blowing it out. "If John Albert ain't ready to let her go, I don't know what to say about that. I ain't about to tussle with no animage. That's a different kind of magic. He's *dark*."

We sat silent a while, drinking our coffee. Finally, I came clean. "I crossed over to talk to him last night."

Now, Big Ginny's eyes went wide. "You did *what* now? He's dangerous! What were you thinking?"

I chewed my lips. "I didn't know he was dangerous," I muttered. "I thought, worst-case scenario, he'd learned backwoods mojo from an ancestor. I thought maybe I could talk him into letting her go. But…"

Big Ginny set her mug down with a thud. "But what? What happened?"

I shivered and recounted the horrifying experience I'd had. The moths, the insects, the frogs, the snakes.

My God, the *snakes*.

Big Ginny blew out a sigh, closing her eyes. "I'm sorry she ain't warn you," she said, shaking her head, rue pulling her mouth into a frown. "That's him all right. He likes them nocturnal creatures the most. Moths, bats, lightning bugs. Well. What's done is done," she said. When she opened her eyes, her expression was careworn. "You okay? How you feel?"

I shrugged. "I feel okay. I mean, physically. I don't think he did anything to me. But I don't think he's going to let Aunt Fat die anytime soon."

My grandmother and I finished our coffees in silence. When Big Ginny finished her cigar, she put it out in the sink and then went out into her vegetable garden without saying another word.

5

I HAD A FEW NIGHTS OFF from work, but the way I'd left things with Aunt Fat sat poorly with me, and I couldn't leave her on her own. So after making sure Big Ginny didn't need me to run any errands or take care of any clients, I loaded up my old iPhone with some raunchy romance novels and went to see my aunt.

When I arrived at the hospice, the sun was just beginning to set, and Jennifer was sitting at the nurse's station, munching on an apple. In the past four months, I'd never seen Jennifer eat anything especially healthy. I raised my eyebrow and she frowned, giving the apple a dirty look. "Margaret put the kibosh on my granola," she grumbled, taking a vindictive bite. "She said I leave *crumbs*. What are you doing here, anyway? You're not on the schedule."

I nodded toward the hallway. "I'm just checking in on my aunt. Bringing her a couple of audiobooks." I held up the iPhone in my hand.

Jennifer nodded. "Oh, yeah. How's she doing?"

I gave half a shrug. "She's still alive," I said, feigning indifference as I glided away.

As I was making my way toward Aunt Fat's corridor, I passed by Mr. Bennett's room, his door slightly ajar. I wasn't in the habit of listening in on other people's conversations, but the voices drifting into the hall were agitated and too loud. It sounded like someone was having an argument. I slowed my pace, straining to listen.

"I *am* listening, Dad, it's just that I think you misunderstand. You *dreamed* that." A pause. "Can I get you something to drink? Some hot tea or something?"

Mr. Bennett's reply was sharp. "You don't know what you're talking about! It wasn't a dream! He was here! I saw him."

I didn't like poking my nose into other people's business, but the conversation was loud and upsetting; if nothing else, I needed to ask them to keep it down. Thankfully, I knew Mr. Bennett and his daughter, Julia, pretty well. He'd been at the hospice for about five months, and he'd already lasted longer than any of us had expected. He was dying of lung cancer. When he came to us, doctors predicted he only had 4 to 6 weeks to live. Which I guess just goes to show what doctors know.

I pushed the door open and entered quietly. When Julia's eyes landed on me, relief flooded her face. "Oh, Kezia, thank God it's you."

"Hey, y'all," I said, forcing a lightness into my voice. "Mr. Bennett? Hey. How are you guys doing?"

Julia's nostrils flared as her eyes flit from me to her father lying in bed with his arms crossed petulantly over his chest. He was facing the other way, refusing to look at us. The old folks got like that sometimes. Ornery.

"Dad thinks someone's been coming into his room," Julia said, hands on her hips. "I've been trying to explain that he probably only dreamed it. But as usual, he doesn't listen."

At this, Mr. Bennett turned to us, a scowl coloring the lines of his face. "It's my *daughter* who won't listen," he huffed. "I've been trying to tell her about the man who keeps coming into my room at night, but she keeps saying it's a nightmare! As if I can't tell a dream from reality! I might have cancer, but I'm not senile!"

I stepped closer to Mr. Bennett's bed and took a seat in the nearby chair. "You've seen a man come into your room? And you're sure it wasn't a nightmare?"

Mr. Bennett's eyes narrowed. "Oh, not you, too. What do I look like to you? Look into my eyes." He took both his index fingers and pulled down on his lower lids, making bug eyes at me. It was all I could do not to laugh. "See these peepers? They work just fine, thank you very much."

It was true that there was nothing wrong with Mr. Bennett's mental faculties, so if he said he saw a man in his room, I had no real reason to discount it. Except, of course, that if a strange man had gone into Mr. Bennett's room, somebody would know about it.

"Tell me about this man," I said.

Mr. Bennett's expression became smug, finally satisfied that someone was taking him seriously. "Well, he always comes at night. When I'm asleep. Which is probably why Julia thinks it's a nightmare," he said, unable to resist the jab. I could almost feel Julia rolling her eyes behind my back.

"He comes when you're asleep?"

Mr. Bennett nodded. "That's right."

"And he wakes you up?"

Now, Mr. Bennett began to fidget, his brow creasing. "Well, no, not exactly. He doesn't wake me up. I see him *in* my sleep."

Julia made an exasperated sound, but I held up a hand to silence her. "So, you see him while you're sleeping, but he's actually here in the room, not inside your head?"

Mr. Bennett nodded. "Yes. I think so, yes."

I nodded. "Okay, keep going. What does he look like?"

"He's old, older than me. Big hands. White hair. And he's always carrying a sweater or something."

I leaned forward, my brows knit in confusion. "He was carrying a *sweater*?"

Mr. Bennett gave a frustrated shrug. "Well, I don't know *exactly* what it is. My wife didn't knit, but that sounds like the sort of thing people knit, right? Sweaters and socks and things? Not that I've ever known a *man* to knit," he said, with more than a hint of disapproval.

The blood drained from my face, though I tried to keep my expression neutral. "Let me repeat back what I think I heard," I drawled. "At night, when you're asleep, a man with big hands and white hair comes into your room carrying a knitting project."

Mr. Bennett gave a definitive nod. "Correct."

My throat had gone dry, and I tried to swallow around the lump that had formed there. "Mr. Bennett, is the man Black?"

Color rose in Mr. Bennett's cheeks and he stammered, breaking eye contact with me. "Well, I don't see color," he said.

Now it was my turn to roll my eyes. "Everybody sees color. Was he? Was he an African-American man?"

Without meeting my eyes, Mr. Bennett nodded again. "He was."

I leaned backward, my mind racing. But before I could quite gather my thoughts, Julia stepped forward, her hand on my shoulder. "Wait, you've *seen* him? Some man really has been coming into my father's room?"

I wasn't sure how to answer this. I drew myself to my feet and beckoned for Julia to follow me into the hallway. "Can I speak to you for just a minute?"

In the hallway, I closed the door softly behind me, keeping my voice low when I said, "No man like that has been at the hospice. However, your father's not the only person who has reported seeing this man."

Julia's expression twisted from concerned to frightened, but I was quick to put my hand on her elbow, a caring gesture that I hoped would calm her nerves. "There's nothing to be afraid of," I assured her. "It's just a nightmare. But the fact that several patients are having the same nightmare means I have some digging to do." I smiled again, and it seemed to do the trick. Anxiety seeped from Julia's face. I pressed on. "Sometimes, when they're near to death, the patients hallucinate. Some of them see dead relatives. And, apparently, some of them see an old Black man knitting a sweater." I broadened my smile to further ease her nerves. "If you ask me, as far as hallucinations go, that one seems pretty mild. I wouldn't worry too much," I said. "But I will look into it. You have my word."

Unexpectedly, Julia leaned forward and pulled me into a quick embrace. "I've always liked you, Kezia," she said. "Thank you. My father might be an insufferable old fool, but I love him very much."

As I pulled away, I nodded. "I understand. I'm actually here to visit my aunt. Another insufferable old fool."

As I watched Julia head back into her father's room, my thoughts were racing. Mr. Bennett had obviously seen John Albert. But if Aunt Fat was right and John Albert was here to punish her and keep her from death, what on earth was he doing bothering Mr. Bennett, who he presumably had never known in life? Had other patients seen him? Could I find out without drawing unwanted attention?

I didn't have any answers, but as I headed toward my aunt's room, I saw something out of the corner of my eye, fluttering near the hallway lights.

Moths.

But when I turned to look directly at them, they were gone.

———

I WAS EXITING the building for the night when I heard someone calling my name. I turned to find Margaret hurrying to catch up with me, wearing the look of someone about to ask for a favor. My heart sank. I wasn't big on favors.

"Kezia," she said. "I've been trying to catch you alone for days. Can I talk to you for a minute? I know you're not on the clock, but this isn't exactly a work matter. A moment?"

I had expected Margaret to direct us back toward the nurse's station, but she escorted me out to the parking lot. Periodically, she glanced over her shoulder, her expression slightly paranoid. I wondered what or who she was looking for.

Or watching out for.

Once we were outside, I hoped Margaret might relax a little, but if anything, she got worse. She fidgeted with her necklace, then ran a hand through her hair. Nervous habits. I wrinkled my brow, gave my head a little shake. "Margaret? Everything okay?"

Margaret chewed her lips and puffed up her cheeks in a heavy sigh. "Everything's fine, I just don't exactly know how to start this conversation." When she saw the look of worry on my face, she chuckled. "Oh, no! Nothing for you to worry about. It's Frankie."

I blinked, surprise rendering me momentarily speechless. Of all the things Margaret could have wanted to talk about, Frankie was nowhere on my list. "Frankie?"

Margaret nodded. "How close are the two of you?"

I rocked back onto my heels, bewildered. "Not close? I don't speak to him outside of work or anything like that. Why do you ask?"

Margaret tapped her lips with her forefinger before answering. "I suppose you've heard by now…"

I nodded. "About Frankie secretly taping the patients? Yeah, I heard. That doesn't sound like Frankie, though."

Margaret made a face. "Well, he did it; he doesn't deny that. Anyway, since I let him go, he's been sending me these text messages," she began. "He says he needs to talk to me and that it's urgent. He says there's something going on here that I need to be aware of. The problem is, some of the families are talking about taking legal action against Frankie and the hospice for violating their privacy. As a result, our lawyers have instructed me not to have any contact with Frankie. I can't even respond to his texts to tell him that I can't speak to him."

I shrugged. "I'm assuming somehow this has to do with me?"

"The other day, his texts changed. I guess he figured out that I wasn't going to respond to him, and the last message he sent said that if I wouldn't talk to him, could I at least give him your number. Which of course I couldn't, but I also wonder…"

She tilted her head back to look at the sky. I recognized the look on her face. Her hands were tied, but Margaret had good senses. Good instincts. She *wanted* to talk to Frankie. Or, more accurately…

"You want me to talk to Frankie and find out what information he has."

Margaret's shoulders sagged in relief. "Yes," she breathed. "That's exactly it. I can't meet with him, but you can. I have no idea what he wants to say, but whatever it is, Frankie isn't really the kind of person to fuck around. This whole situation stinks, to be perfectly honest. He put me in a bad position."

I nodded. "What he did wasn't just illegal, it's also unethical. You did what you had to do."

Margaret frowned. "I did, but it's been nagging me ever since we found those cameras. What was he doing? What was he looking for? You'll never convince me that Frankie was just being a perv. I know Michael says you can't know what gets someone off just by working with them, but I feel like I have a good read on people. Frankie was *looking* for something. I need you to help me find out what it was."

I shifted my weight and crossed my arms over my chest. "Yeah, I can do that. Why don't you give me his number? I'll see if I can meet up with him for lunch or something over the next couple of days. That work?"

Margaret made an appreciative sound as she fished her phone from her pocket. "I'm texting you his contact information now," she said. My phone buzzed as it received her message. "There. Done. Listen, I know this is a weird request, and I don't ask it lightly. So I really appreciate you doing this for me."

I nodded and gave her an expression like it wasn't a big deal, but in truth, I had a lot of questions. Why had Frankie asked for *me*? I had been friendly with him when we worked together, but no more than any of the other nurses. I couldn't imagine why he'd ask for me. Unless…

My heart skipped a beat. Unless he specifically wanted to talk to me not as a friend or a coworker, but as a necromancer.

"I gotta go," I said, backing toward my car. "But I'll be sure to let you know what I find out."

Margaret dipped her head in appreciation before turning back and heading inside.

I got into the car and sat behind the wheel for a few minutes before turning on the ignition. Strange things were happening at hospice. Frankie putting cameras in the patients' rooms. John Albert haunting and torturing the guests. None of it was anything I couldn't handle, but it all sat wrong with me. I felt like pieces of this puzzle were still missing.

But whatever those pieces were, I wouldn't find them sitting in my car. So I started up the engine and headed home.

LATER THAT NIGHT, after I was showered and ready for bed, I turned out the lights in my bedroom and sat down to my altar. I lit my ancestor candles, anointed myself with rose attar oil, and lit a cone of incense. I closed my eyes and focused my thoughts on my mother.

I couldn't see her face. I had few photos of her, and in most, her face was turned away from the camera. I knew a few key things about her: she liked to sing, she was good at math, and she adored Big Ginny. It wasn't much to go on, yet it should have been enough. I focused on her name, on her DNA in my blood, on the lineage we shared. I slowed my breathing and tried to conjure her with my will.

But my monkey brain kept springing away from my intention, demanding that I think about the situation with Aunt Fat. Each time the thought came, I pushed it gently away, returning my intention to my mother. But no sooner did I reach for the death current, cajoling it into carrying me to the other side, than my thoughts would once again slip away from me, returning to Aunt Fat lying terrified in her bed, crying and begging me to stop John Albert.

Frustrated, I opened my eyes and tilted my head back. "*Fine*," I huffed. "Fine, we'll deal with John Albert. I haven't found my mother in years; what's another night?"

I stood up and went to my closet, where I dug out a fresh black candle. Unlike Big Ginny, I wasn't comfortable putting words on other people. Binding others or otherwise preventing them from working magic was a big deal. If the universe examined my intentions and found them wanting, every action that I took could be turned around and used against me. So I took directed magic, spells cast on other people, very seriously.

But I had seen with John Albert could do. And while I didn't believe Aunt Fat was precisely in danger, she wasn't exactly resting peacefully, was she? It was a strange position to be in. Most of the time, people feared death. They wanted to keep their loved ones alive. They wanted to spend more time with them. It was why families loved working with Camille. She could give those families more time, another smile, one more precious moment to store away in their memories. More comforts to rely on when the world was grim.

But my case was exactly the opposite. I didn't fear Aunt Fat's death—I feared Aunt Fat's *life*. I feared her pain, her suffering, her separation from the friends and family waiting to embrace her on the other side. I didn't want my aunt to keep living. She didn't want it, either. Fat had lived a good life, and it was time for her to move on.

And my job as a necromancer—and as a trained death worker—was to make sure that happened as peacefully as possible.

A true protection ritual or a proper banishing rite would be preferable to anything quick and dirty, but both of those spells required me to go to the hospice, something I wasn't willing to do at this hour. But I could do some preliminary work at my altar. I prayed from the book of Psalms as I lit the black candle. And as I hovered my hands over the flame, letting the heat radiate through my hands and up my arms and into my heart, I imagined John Albert, his dark, beautiful skin, his glowing white hair, his strange, wild, animal magic.

And then I began to cast. To put words on him.

Big Ginny would absolutely throttle me if she knew what I was doing. She feared John Albert, which meant I should fear him. If I were smart, I'd wait until morning when I could go down to Necro Sis and ask Opal for help. But while I wasn't exactly excited about another run-in with him, I wasn't really afraid.

But no, that wasn't true, was it? I *was* afraid. But I was also impatient, and my monkey brain wasn't going to let me sleep until I dealt at least an initial blow to the deceased animage.

Resigning myself to working a curse before bedtime, I cut my finger with a lancet and dribbled blood onto a black cloth. I pressed cowslip blossoms into the cloth, drenching them with my blood as I recited my enemy's name. I tied knots into the cloth. I envisioned his back, walking away, assholes and elbows growing smaller in the distance.

I almost laughed.

But then a sound caught my attention.

My head jerked up and my jaw went slack. There, standing in the corner of my room, was John Albert.

I was too stunned to make a sound. How could he *be* here? Big Ginny kept wards on the house. No person who meant us harm could cross the brick dust she laid at every entrance.

But then a memory bubbled to the forefront of my brain. Jennifer's face dipped in shame, telling Margaret the patients were only seeing crickets in their rooms. *Everybody gets crickets,* she'd said.

Everybody. Including us.

And crickets could probably cross Big Ginny's brick dust, whether or not they meant us harm.

And animages could possess crickets.

I pressed a hand to my mouth to keep from shouting as I scrambled to my feet, reaching for a ritual dagger I kept near my bed. But my hands were shaking too badly to grab onto it. It slipped through my fingers, clattering to the floor, and before I could retrieve it, John Albert lunged at me.

Just like at the bayou, I heard the scream of insects in my ears, the frantic beating of a bird's wings against my face. I felt talons on my skin, scales wrapping around my legs, spiders skittering over my shoulders.

It's not real, I told myself. *Focus!* But even as I tried to convince myself that it was only a hallucination, John Albert reached for me, grabbing my face, his hand the size of my head, his fingertips sinking into my flesh. I was paralyzed beneath his grip. I could scarcely breathe I was so terrified. And then his voice, deep as thunder and just as commanding, saying, "You dare to put words on me?"

I flailed under his grasp, trying to escape his grip, but he was so much stronger than me. He pulled me towards him and with his free hand, pressed the air from my lungs as his grip tightened around my throat.

If I let him, he would kill me.

But it wasn't my physical body he wanted. It was my ability to cast spells. My spirit. And if my spirit slipped away from my body, he might let my body go.

It was a ballsy move, but it was the only play I had. Sucking in the deepest breath I could manage through my panic, I threw my consciousness out to the universe, howling for the death current to do my bidding, and when I felt its energy moving through me, rippling through my body, I latched onto it, commanding it to jolt me through the veil. I landed on the far shore with such force that I fell immediately to my hands and knees, my brain swimming, my stomach sick. I'd never gone through the veil so recklessly. But I had to escape my body. It was the only way.

But even here, I wasn't safe. Even though I landed on the shore instead of the bayou, I couldn't trust that John Albert couldn't get to me. I scrambled to my feet, running, calling out for my ancestors to find me and protect me.

Then, in the distance, I heard it.

The chirping of crickets, the screeching of bats. The sounds were getting louder.

John Albert was coming for me.

With tears streaming down my face, I ran as fast as my legs could carry me, my feet sinking into the sand, but even as I ran, I felt the chill of his breath on the back of my neck, the slither of reptiles on my heels. Biting flies attacked my scalp, my neck, and skittered down between my buttocks.

Out of breath and with so few options, I spun on my heel, my arms outstretched. "What do you want from us?" I screamed. "Why won't you just leave her alone? You can't keep her alive forever; no one can do that! You have to leave her alone!"

John Albert was in front of me now, but made no move to advance. His eyes were deep pools of black, his frown full of threat. He pointed a gnarled finger at my face. "Stay away from her," he said, his voice all gravel and glass. "All of you. She's mine, you hear? You stay away."

I opened my mouth to retort that she didn't belong to him, that she was my family, and I was bound to protect her. But before I could get the words out, I awoke in my physical body, shivering and drenched in sweat. My eyes flicked to the ceiling where shadows of winged insects played against the light. And although I couldn't see him, I heard John Albert's voice whispering in my ear. "I am everywhere," he said.

I pressed my hands to my ears and squeezed my eyes shut. *No, no, no, this isn't happening,* I thought. *I'm imagining things. I—*

The click of the air conditioner turning on pulled me out of my impending hysterics. I opened my eyes and took a deep breath of cool air. But something was wrong.

When I'd crossed over, I'd been in my bedroom. Now, I was lying on my back in the hallway. Somehow my physical body had moved when my consciousness was on the other side.

But that was impossible.

Impossible, maybe. But nevertheless, there I was, in the hallway. And only moments before I was on the other side. And only moments before that?

What was happening?

I cursed. *I've never moved while on the other side before. Never! I wish I could have seen it! I wish I could —*

But that wasn't true, was it? It *had* happened before. The night in my aunt's room, the first time I'd run into John Albert.

A lightbulb went off in my head. Was that why Frankie had recorded the patients? Had he noticed strange movements, unusual ambulations, sleepwalking? Was he trying to capture something like this on video? Did Frankie know about the dreams, the hallucinations, the spectral night visits? Was that why he asked for me?

I wobbled to my feet and returned to my bedroom where I snatched my phone off the charger and dashed a quick message to Frankie. It read: "I need to talk to you. When's the soonest we can meet?"

Then, I pretty much passed out.

6

DAYS LATER, I WAS BACK at the hospice, which was busier than usual. When I entered the building, I only saw one person sitting at the nurse's station. Jennifer was munching on a bag of chips—apparently, she was over apples. "Where is everybody?" I asked.

Jennifer's eyes went wide as she covered her mouth to hide her chewing. "Oh my gosh, Kezia. It's been crazy around here. We've lost like *six* patients in the past couple of days."

My eyes went wide with surprise. "That many? Why, what happened?"

Jennifer shrugged, gesturing about wildly. "I mean, nothing! I mean, nothing weird happened or anything. It was just all of a sudden, everybody kind of..." Jennifer leaned forward, lowering her voice. "They just all kicked the bucket one right after another. Like their batteries all ran out at the same time."

"Don't say things like that," I replied automatically. "Who? Who did we lose?"

Jennifer ticked the names off on her fingers. "Mrs. Lewis, Mr. Bennett, Mr. Landry, Ms. Kendall, and Mrs. Vasquez."

"Oh, no," I breathed, my hand going to my throat. "We lost Mr. Bennett?"

Jennifer's expression was solemn. "Julia was with him," she said.

"That's good," I muttered, though the thought brought me little comfort. His loss stabbed me in the heart. I had just seen him. I had promised Julia I'd get to the bottom of his nightmares. Had I failed them? Or did Mr. Bennett's life simply follow its natural course?

Jennifer leaned back and blew out a puff of air. "Anyway, I think Margaret wanted you to get started changing the sheets in Mrs. Vasquez's room. I already did the others."

I shrugged out of my jacket and put my things away before heading to the linen closet. I was rounding the corner, about to step inside when I nearly plowed into Camille. The other woman drew up short, her hand pressed against her chest as she gasped. "Oh," she breathed. "I didn't see you coming! You startled me."

She startled me, too, and not just because I'd almost crashed into her. Camille looked terrible. Where she usually looked so bright and vibrant, her skin was now a sickly gray with dark circles under her eyes that made her face look hollowed out. Her lips were chapped and pale; even her hair was in dull disarray. She looked as though she hadn't slept or eaten in days.

"Sorry," I mumbled. "I need to watch where I'm going." I hesitated. "Hey, are you okay? Is there anything I can help you with?"

I knew better than to tell her she looked like something the cat dragged in. That was the sort of thing people said presumably out of empathy, but it rarely helped. Who wants to be told they look like shit when they can't do anything about it?

Camille bit her lips and tried to smile, but the expression faltered. "I'm having a rough time," she admitted. "We lost a bunch of patients recently." Tears sprang to her eyes, and she blinked them back, wiping furiously at her dripping nose. "It's just—you know, work is the only thing I have. When they die—especially so suddenly—it feels like a failure." She dropped her chin to her chest. "I didn't even get to say goodbye."

I touched her lightly on the forearm. "Camille, you know you can't keep them alive forever. And that's okay. Losing patients is part of the job. Some might even say it *is* the job."

A single tear escaped Camille's eye, but she brushed it away quickly, again trying on that smile. "I know. I'm being ridiculous. I think it's a combination of things. First, I lost Diablo, then several of my favorite patients. It's just a lot. But I'll be okay. Thank you for asking."

I nodded. "I'm sure Margaret will give you some time off if you ask. You have to take care of yourself. There's no way you can do this work when you're teetering on the edge like this."

Again, Camille nodded, offering that fake-it-till-you-make-it smile. "You're right. I'll do that. I'll take some time. Thanks, Kezia. I'll talk to you later."

I gathered the linens I needed and made my way to Mrs. Vasquez's room. I changed the sheets, mopped the floors, and was heading toward the laundry room when I ran into Margaret. She looked harried. Her skin was sallow, her eyes bloodshot. Her nose was red and raw, like she'd been blowing it too hard and too frequently.

I never saw Margaret like this. She was usually all steel and ice. Seeing her hollowed out broke something inside me.

"Margaret? Is everything okay?" I asked.

Margaret shook her head, squeezing her eyes shut. "This

place has been a madhouse lately. I swear, it's enough to drive a person to drink."

I grunted. "Any patient in particular?"

Margaret waved a hand vaguely. "Mr. Paulson. He's been having nightmares. I'm tempted to give him sedatives in the evening, but I don't know. I want to talk to his family about it first, but I haven't been able to reach them."

"Nightmares?" My stomach flipped. "What kind of nightmares?"

Again, Margaret shrugged, uninterested. "I don't know. You heard that we lost six patients recently? I just really don't have time for theatrics. If you want to go talk to him, feel free. He seems to like you."

I nodded. "Okay. Let me know if you need anything else."

"Well, actually," she said, stepping nearer and lowering her voice. "Have you talked to Frankie yet?"

I shook my head. "I sent him a text, but he hasn't replied. I'm hesitant to follow up."

Margaret thought for a moment before waving her hand, dismissing it. "Couldn't have been too important then," she said, faking a breezy smile. "Thanks for trying."

After dumping the linens off in the laundry room, I found Mr. Paulson sitting at the little table by the window in his room, playing a game of solitaire. When I came in, he looked up and smiled, his expression brightening. "Haven't seen you in a while," he said. "Where they been keeping you?"

I smiled. "They've been keeping me away from you because they didn't want me enchanted by your wily charms," I teased. I slid into the chair across from him, tapping the table with a forefinger. "Who's winning?"

Mr. Paulson groaned. "I hate it when you people treat me

like an infant. I don't mind playing solitaire, but I'd much rather play a game of chess. Do you play chess?"

I gave a rueful shake of my head. "Nope. The only thing I know about chess is that the horsey moves in an L."

Mr. Paulson scowled. "It's not a horsey; it's a knight."

I clucked my tongue. "Okay, the knight then. Like I said, that's all I know. So, listen. This isn't just a friendly visit."

Again, Mr. Paulson groaned. "It never is. You're not here to prick me, are you? Can't you let a man die in peace?"

The question was ironic, and I couldn't help but chuckle. "I'm not here to stick you with anything. Besides, you look pretty spry for a geezer. Doesn't look to me like you're dying anytime soon. I want to talk to you about the nightmares you've been having."

Now, Mr. Paulson looked up from his game of solitaire as though I'd finally said something interesting. "Nobody wants to talk about the nightmares. Margaret just keeps threatening to give me sedatives if I keep having them."

"Margaret's not gonna give you any sedatives without permission. Besides, you probably don't need them. You're not the only one having nightmares."

Mr. Paulson leaned in closer, steepling his fingers beneath his chin. "Really? Tell me more."

I shook my head. "No, you tell me first. What are the nightmares about?"

Mr. Paulson pushed back from the table and stood up, linking his hands behind his back. He marched across the room and stopped in the corner, still facing the walls. "He stands right here," he said.

"Who does?"

"The spider man."

I hesitated, sure that I didn't understand what I just heard. "Spider-Man?"

Mr. Paulson gave a definitive nod. "That's what I said."

Wearily, I pressed my palm to my forehead and let my eyes flutter closed. "I don't understand. You've been having nightmares about a superhero?"

Now, Mr. Paulson turned around, his cheeks ruddy and his expression incredulous. "Not Spider-Man, you idiot. The spider man. A man who turns into a spider. He stands here, weaving his web. Like he's trying to catch something. Trying to catch a fly."

That made more sense, at least. "What does he look like?"

"African-American. Dark skin. White hair. Mean-looking sonofabitch. You're not gonna tell Margaret I said that, are you? She started making me use a swear jar." He pointed to a glass on his nightstand. "One quarter every time I say a curse word. At my age, I should be allowed to say as many curse words as I want. Fuck Margaret," he said. I was certain he said it just for shock value. I knew for a fact Mr. Paulson quite liked Margaret.

"No, we're gonna leave Margaret out of this. Forget about her for a minute. So you're telling me an African-American man stands in the corner of your room and turns into a spider?"

Mr. Paulson tucked his chin against his chest. "And weaves a web," he repeated. "That's what I said."

I stood up and walked over to where Mr. Paulson stood, clapping him gently on the shoulder. "I see. That's what other people have been seeing, too," I said. When Mr. Paulson didn't look convinced, I lowered my voice and added, "Including me."

That piqued his interest. "You've seen him?"

I nodded. "Yes, but don't tell Margaret. She hasn't seen him, and she might not believe us. So we can keep this just between us? You and me?"

Mr. Paulson pretended to zip his lips shut.

"Okay," I smiled. "Great. Thank you. Now, listen. The good news is I have an idea about how to stop it." I paused. "At least for a while."

Mr. Paulson frowned. "What's the bad news?"

I shook my head. "I don't have any bad news."

The old man's frown deepened. "Well, you just said the good news was you had an idea, but you said it like there was bad news, too."

I shrugged. "I don't know what to tell you. I don't have bad news."

Mr. Paulson rolled his eyes. "You don't make any sense," he grumbled. "But at any rate, I'm sick of the spiders in my room. Crickets, too. I thought they were gonna fumigate this place! But every night, there's more bugs!"

I pursed my lips together. "Are there? I thought they *did* bring in an exterminator."

Mr. Paulson crossed his arms over his chest. "If they did, they missed *my* room, goddammit."

He huffed, then walked over to the swear jar, dug a coin from a drawer, and threw it into the glass.

I rolled my eyes. Mr. Paulson did love his theatrics. "I've got to run, but I'm gonna look into these nightmares for you. But you gotta be nice to Margaret. She's having a rough time. Deal?"

I held out my hand, but Mr. Paulson ignored it. "I don't make deals," he said. "But if you can stop the nightmares from happening, I'll pay you five dollars. Ten if you get rid of the bugs."

As I HEADED BACK into the hall, I pulled out my phone and tapped out a text message to Big Ginny. "Regarding our friend the animage. What would happen, in theory, if you killed an insect while he was possessing it?"

I hit send.

Back at the nurse's station, Jennifer was peering at her computer monitor, her brow furrowed. "Mr. Paulson's coming up on the end of his six months already. Do you think his family will take him home if his insurance won't pay for his care any longer?"

I shrugged. "What choice will they have?"

Jennifer wiped crumbs from her chin. "None, I guess. It's too bad people can't choose where and how they die," she said. "I mean, sure, you can decide you want to die at home, or you can decide you want to die in hospice. At least in theory. But really, what say do any of us really have over that? It feels like our final time on earth is determined by someone else. Doesn't that seem wrong to you? Shouldn't we get to decide how we spend our final moments?"

"I can't argue with any of that," I said. "But the universe has never been fair."

"I think I'd rather die in hospice than at home," she continued, speaking more to herself than to me. "I mean, the idea of dying at home seems better at first. You're in your own bed, surrounded by your own things, in a place that has been your home and your comfort for a long time. But the thing is, unless your family can afford to get you a full-time live-in nurse? Then they have to take care of you. And then slowly, over time, they start to resent you. Or even if they don't start to resent you, they start to think of you differently. You stop being their awesome grandmother or aunt or mom. You start to just be a patient, another chore that they have to put up with at the end of their already exhausting workdays. I don't want that," Jennifer said with a shake of her head. "I want my family to be my family to the end. And if that means that I have to die in a hospital or a place like this? Then so be it."

My phone buzzed, and I fished it from my pocket, surprised to see that Big Ginny had already responded. Her message read, "Long term? Nothing. But short-term, might vex him enough to tie up his magic. He'll have to go through the actions to disconnect himself from the horse. Sometimes can take a while."

The horse was what hoodoo workers called the person or animal being possessed by a foreign spirit. Big Ginny's answer was exactly what I wanted to hear. Excitement bubbled in my veins as I typed back, "Long enough to let Aunt Fat die?"

Three dots appeared, meaning Big Ginny was typing. I held my breath in anticipation.

"Worth a try. Gonna piss him off, though."

I blew out my breath, hardly able to believe my luck. "Not coming home, then. Gonna eat dinner out, and then coming back to the hospice. Might be here all night. Don't wait up."

Three dots again. I waited for the response. This time, the message read, "I never do."

Smiling, I put my phone away and turned to Jennifer. "You hungry? I'm thinking about stepping out to get dinner. You're off in an hour, right?"

Jennifer turned to me, an embarrassed blush blooming in her cheeks. "Yeah, but I can't go out with you tonight. I'm sorry. It's just that..." She chewed her lips. "I've been seeing you a lot lately. And..."

She looked quickly down into her lap, and I understood.

She was afraid of the blues. "I get it," I said, forcing myself to smile. "No, really, I get it. No hard feelings."

My phone buzzed again, and assuming it must be Big Ginny again, I took it out to check the message. But the message wasn't from my grandmother.

It was from Frankie.

I tapped on the message. "Been out of town. Sorry. I can meet you tomorrow. Does that work?"

Holding my breath, I tapped back, "How about coffee? Noon?" I typed in an address and waited for response.

I didn't have to wait long. His reply was, "Sounds good. See you then."

I tucked my phone back into my pocket and retrieved the rest of my belongings. My shift was over, and I needed to run some errands before I went to hang out with Aunt Fat for the rest of the night. I finally had some direction about how to stop John Albert's harassment and to allow my aunt to finally pass over into the afterlife peacefully.

But I was going to need a little bit of help to get there.

Necro Sis was a necromancer-owned magical supply shop a few neighborhoods away. The shop proprietor, Opal, was a friend of the family and a necromancer with the Godsend. She was skinny and dark-skinned and wore her platinum white hair in bantu knots all over her head. You couldn't not love Opal. Black folks from miles around came to her to receive their gifts.

The bells above the door tinkled as I entered, and when Opal saw me coming in, her whole face lit up. She flashed me a huge, surprised smile and pulled me into a bear hug that I gratefully returned. "Queen Kezia! Girl, I ain't seen you in a minute. How's Big Ginny? How's you?"

"We both good," I said. "You? How's business?"

Opal gestured to the empty room. "Hopping," she said with a sarcastic grin.

I clicked my tongue and gave my head a shake. "Folks is gettin lazy," I lamented. "I remember when getting a gift was as important as going to church. Well, it'll be Halloween before you know it." I smiled, and thankfully, Opal joined me in the expression. "Yo. I need to stock up on some supplies. You got any of that third-eye tea?"

Opal sucked her teeth, rolling her eyes. "Girl, what you take me for? Come on." She beckoned for me to follow her over to her bulk herb section. Rows and rows of crushed herbs lined the walls. She plucked a glass container from the shelf and set it on the table. "How much you want?"

I shrugged. "Might as well give me enough for a half-dozen servings."

Opal dug the plastic scoop into the crushed herbs and poured the contents into a small Ziploc baggie, which she then handed to me. "By itself, that tastes like shit," Opal advised. "If you want, I got this bomb-ass honey powder you can mix directly with the herbs. It adds sweetness and a mellow flavor."

I nodded. "Sounds good."

Opal plucked a tin from a shelf and handed it to me. "Put 2 teaspoons of the crushed herbs into a tea ball and add as much honey powder as you like. Then add boiling water and steep for about 3 to 4 minutes. You should be good to go." Opal cocked an eyebrow in my direction, her head listing sideways. "You don't usually buy third-eye tea. You tryna see something in particular?" She leaned forward in mock conspiracy. "You looking for ghosts?" She fluttered her hands by her platinum bantu knots, making fun of me.

I feigned a chuckle and shook my head. "Not ghosts," I said. But I didn't elaborate further.

"A'ight, well listen, that stuff is strong. It's got mugwort in it. The closer you drink it to your bedtime, the more powerful it is. You'll probably have intense visions, but don't be afraid. You won't see anything the Universe doesn't want you to see."

She gave me a pointed look to make sure I understood, and when she was satisfied, led me over to the cash register where she rang me up and I paid with cash. As I was about to leave, Opal called out, "Queen Kee. Girl. You want a gift? Or do you already have one on you?"

I hesitated. How long had it been since I'd gone to another necromancer for a gift? In the old days, I was religious about going, hoping I'd receive a gift that helped me find my mother and ignite my own Godsend. But when years went by and nothing happened, I quit.

"I don't have one on me," I said finally. Only one gift could be active at a time, and a new gift could only be granted once the previous had worn off. You couldn't replace one with another. "I guess it's been awhile. Okay, yeah."

Opal placed her hands on either side of my face. Within a moment, I saw her hands vibrate with a soft, magenta glow. My cheeks grew warm under her touch, and my pulse quickened. When she pulled them away, she smiled. "Well? Which did you get?"

The knowledge bloomed inside me like a rose, sure and heady and strong. "Clear thinking," I said with a smile.

"Sometimes called 'Connect the dots,' it's the ability to see things as they are and make accurate connections between known information," Opal recited. She'd been doing this a long time. "Eh, not an especially exciting gift, but not worthless. Use it well," she advised. "And don't be a stranger."

AFTER DINNER, I made my way back to the hospice. I found Jennifer in the break room nibbling on a bowl of salad.

I sauntered past her, frowning over my shoulder as I headed toward the hot water maker. "I thought you were going home." I paused, glancing down at her meal. "That looks…good?"

Jennifer stabbed her salad with too much force. "Margaret asked me to stay for another hour. She gave me her dinner as a consolation prize." She sighed, plopped her chin in her hand. "No wonder Margaret's so skinny. This shit is rabbit food."

I chuckled and pulled the honey powder from the brown paper bag I brought from Opal's. "Here," I said, pushing the tin towards her. "You might like this. It's a natural sweetener. Seems like the sort of thing foodies would appreciate, so I thought of you. It won't make that salad taste any better," I lamented, "but maybe in your coffee later…?"

This seemed to lighten Jennifer's mood somewhat. She lifted the lid and sniffed. "Oooh, that smells *good*," she breathed. "Maybe I'll try some later. Thanks."

Jennifer went back to angrily stabbing her dinner while I prepared my third-eye tea the way Opal had instructed me, replacing the honey powder with regular sugar. "See ya," I said as I headed for Aunt Fat's room.

She was asleep when I got there. Settling into the armchair on the opposite side of the room, I pulled my e-reader from my bag and got comfortable. When it was cool enough, I took a sip of the mugwort tea. I grimaced. It was still bitter and tasted like shit.

I decided sipping it was just an exercise in torture. I drank it as quickly as I could without burning my lips and tongue. When it was finished, I set the mug on the table and waited.

I had a theory about what the old people had been seeing. I remembered Jennifer telling me that the patients had been complaining of bugs and that Margaret had called in an exterminator. All the time I'd been here, we'd never had a bug problem before. So that got me thinking: were the bugs there because Jennifer left her crumbs everywhere? Or was there something more sinister behind their presence?

If the bugs resulted from John Albert's meddling, maybe I could do something about it myself. Mr. Paulson said that John Albert appeared as both a man and a spider. If that were true, maybe he came to Aunt Fat in the same way. As a spider. It made sense: it explained why he was always knitting. He was weaving a web. Catching his victims like flies. Knitting the threads of their lives, longer, and longer, and longer…

The thought made me shudder.

But if Big Ginny and I were right, all I needed to do was kill him when he was in his transformed state. It was a short-term fix, to be sure. Once he realized I had killed him, he would just extract his consciousness from the horse and integrate all of his pieces back into his primary self on the other side. But that would take some time.

Though not a lot of time.

I looked over at Aunt Fat, at her steady, even breathing. She looked peaceful, but not like she was about to die. I didn't feel any buzzing or throbbing in my hands. What I was doing tonight might not work. But I had to give it a shot.

And that's where the tea came in. None of this would mean anything if I killed an ordinary house spider. I had to make sure I killed the right spider. And for that, I needed to see through its disguise. Third-eye tea would allow me to see what my regular eyes could not: magic, spirits, enchantments, things like that. It would allow me to see with my soul.

The tea took effect just as I was nodding off. The chair was uncomfortable, and I squirmed, trying to find a good position. But just as I was getting grumpy and beginning to wonder if this had been a dumb idea, I caught a flutter of movement from the corner of my eye.

I saw the spider first, an eight-legged nuisance that skittered across the floor. But the shadow it threw on the long wall was man-shaped: tall, brooding, and foreboding. My breath caught as I watched John Albert move, at once a spider and a man-like thing, and the image was so unnatural it made my skin crawl.

But though I watched him with fascinated revulsion, he didn't see me. He was focused on Aunt Fat snoring softly in her bed. Even when I rose from my chair, the furniture squeaking as I stood, he didn't turn towards me. I retrieved my mug, empty now, and held it behind my back as I took tentative, quiet steps toward the spider. And then, swallowing down my repulsion, I leapt.

I plopped the mug upside down over the spider. The moment the arachnid was trapped, a blast of fury struck me. John Albert's voice screamed in my ears. "What the hell are you doing? Let me out! You don't know what you're dealing with!"

"Neither do you," I hissed. "Six patients passed over recently. Despite your best efforts, six people died peacefully, just as they're supposed to do. You're not as strong as you thought. You—"

Something shimmered in the corner of my eye. I stopped mid-sentence, turning my eyes to the glinting light. Strung across the room from wall to wall was a labyrinth of translucent, glittering threads that pulsed with a neon green glow. Their interconnections were intricate and beautiful, at once mesmerizing and terrible. Staring at them, I knew instinctively what they were. These were John Albert's webs. This was the twisted magic he'd been weaving on his visits.

A dim memory of Camille snipping stray threads from her scrubs bloomed in my mind. "I just rip them out," Jennifer had said as she watched Camille meticulously remove the threads. "What's the big deal?" But Camille had frowned, shaking her head. "That's not the way to do it. You have to care for your things correctly, so they'll last you a long time." She slid the scissors into Margaret's desk drawer and brushed the threads to the floor.

My breath caught in my throat. *Margaret has scissors in her desk drawer.*

In a trance, I slipped out of Aunt Fat's room, glided into Margaret's office, and removed the scissors from her desk.

Don't! John Albert's voice was furious but strangled. Trapping his horse had weakened him, just as Big Ginny had predicted. Invigorated by my small win, I gave the scissors a try. Open, shut. Open, shut. They worked just fine.

I grinned to myself. Then I followed the threads.

To my right, there were threads leading into Mr. Paulson's room. Inside, the webs were complex and dazzling, just as they were in Aunt Fat's room. I stood on my tiptoes, reaching toward the ceiling, the point of the scissors angled skyward. I snapped the two blades together.

Snip.

Next, I wandered to Mrs. Lao's room. Mrs. Lao should have died weeks ago. Elation bubbled in my veins as I took the scissors to the webs that surrounded her like a cocoon. Snip.

In my mugwort-tea-induced semi-tripped-out state, I

followed threads throughout the whole building, snipping strands wherever I found them, watching them flutter to the ground with grim satisfaction. With each thread I cut, I felt a wave of anger, a pulse of fury. John Albert didn't like my releasing the patients from his hold over them. Too bad. I was a necromancer, and I was here to protect my patients from suffering and grief. It was my job to lead them towards a gentle death and the eternal peace that awaited them on the other side.

I snipped every thread I found until they all lay in heaps on the ground. Aunt Fat was still sleeping when I finished destroying all the webs in her room. I watched her for a moment, wondering if she were close, if she were drawing nearer to death. But when I didn't sense her mortic energy, no impending sense of transition, I turned to the spider trapped underneath the mug.

I lifted the mug and as the spider tried to scurry away, I squashed him beneath my heel.

7

THE NEXT MORNING, I was scheduled for a short shift. Camille, who usually worked nights, was sitting at the nurse's station doing shoulder rolls and stretching her neck. When she saw me, she flashed me a bright smile.

"Hey!" I said. "Good morning. How's it going?"

Camille flipped her hair over her shoulder, her smile widening. "I am doing *so much better*," she cooed. "Can't you tell? Don't I look better?"

She did. In fact, she looked amazing. Her cheeks had a rosy glow, and the circles under her eyes had vanished. Her hair was sleek and well-manicured. She looked like herself again. "You really do. What's your secret? Don't say Botox," I warned. "I can't afford that shit on my part-time salary."

Camille laughed, and it sounded genuine. "No, nothing like that. I took your advice. I asked Margaret for some time off. Even just thinking about taking a vacation made me feel better. I went home early yesterday and got a lot of sleep, and then right before work this morning I stopped by the shelter and I picked up a new puppy." Her smile widened. "So yeah. I'm feeling a lot better. Thanks for asking."

"Well, good," I said. "Have you seen my aunt today? How's she doing?"

Camille's smile faltered. "It's good you're here," she said, her voice dipping toward condolence. "She's not well. She seems...I don't know. Afraid." Camille sucked in a breath, tossed her bangs from her eyes. "I'm sorry. Should I not have said that?"

I swallowed, hands clenching at my sides. "No, it's okay. Anything else?"

"I sat with her a little while this morning. I thought it might help."

I offered Camille a grateful smile, but it felt fake and immediately slipped from my face as I hurried to Aunt Fat's room. I reached out with my senses, feeling for John Albert's presence. I didn't feel him there among the shadows. And yet, as soon as I stepped inside my aunt's room, I knew something was wrong.

The smells of death that I had become so accustomed to were not only lessened, but they had a strange quality to them. They smelled musty and darkly floral. There was something else, too. The death current felt agitated. Like a lion pacing in a cage or a dog yowling before a storm. Like it was warning me of something to come.

Frowning, I stepped over to my aunt's bed. At the sight of her, my heart dropped into my stomach. She looked terrible. She was scowling in her sleep, like she was in pain. Her hands clenched the sheet at her chest, and her upper lip twitched. Her skin was ash gray and her lips dry.

She looked close to death. With all my experience, I could safely say that this was a person who was supposed to pass over. And yet, the death current wasn't carrying her away. Her mortic energy wasn't materializing.

It was like she was stuck in a state of pre-death, tortured and in pain and unable to find peace.

She looked like John Albert still had a hold over her.

This doesn't make sense! I cursed inwardly, frustration rolling off me in waves. I had snipped all the threads. I had crushed any insect I had found. Sure, I knew that killing the spider wouldn't thwart John Albert forever, but the effects should have lasted longer than one night!

Our plan of attack wasn't working. Aunt Fat was still suffering. Apparently, I needed more than my own meager magic to counteract John Albert.

That revelation put a damper on the rest of my shift. I performed my duties with a fake smile, running through the motions, but my heart wasn't in it. I didn't make small talk with the patients. I didn't ask them how they were feeling or how they'd slept. I fluffed pillows, I poured glasses of water, I and I let people know that their loved ones were on their way. But I offered no other consolations. No humanity.

By the time my shift was over, I was angry and agitated and wanted nothing more than to go home. But I'd made that coffee date with Frankie, and I wasn't a flake. And besides, I was curious what he knew. So I made my way to the coffee shop.

Frankie was already there when I arrived. He offered me a nervous smile as I slid into the seat across from him, his fingers drumming on the table. He was a good-looking kid, even though he had a tendency to wear too much eyeliner. His long, black bangs fell in a swoop across his eyes and he kept pushing them aside. I wondered why he didn't just cut them shorter.

"Sorry I'm late," I said. "It's good to see you. You look good. How are things?"

Frankie shrugged, throwing a glance out the window rather than meeting my eyes. "Not bad. You?"

I nodded. "Yeah, I'm good. Work's good. How's your family?"

He sucked his teeth, making a shooing motion with his hand. "Good, I guess, though they are on my ass about finding a job." He rolled his eyes. "My folks keep trying to convince me to go back to nursing school and get a real degree." He said these last words with air quotes around them. "They don't think being a certified nursing assistant is good enough. *It limits your job search possibilities, Frankie*," he whined, no doubt mimicking his mother's voice. He gave a shrug and made a face. "I mean, you know, she's not wrong, but like, I don't got that nursing school money, you know? Plus, that shit takes years to finish. I don't have time for all that. The only thing I want to invest in for that long is my music."

The last thing I wanted to talk about was Frankie's music career, so I diverted toward safer waters. "You could always take out a loan for nursing school," I suggested. "I mean, if you wanted to go."

"I guess," he said. But it wasn't convincing.

I sighed and folded my hands on the table. "So, listen. Margaret asked me to meet with you. She's not allowed to communicate with you. Something about her lawyers. I don't know. But she does want to know what you have to say. I guess you asked her for my number?"

Frankie folded his arms over his chest, his leg bouncing under the table causing it to shake. I tried to ignore the soft clatter of silverware against cheap coffee mugs. "You know she fired me because I was recording the patients," he said. "I guess you've heard that, right?"

I nodded. "Yeah."

Frankie took in a sharp breath. "I'd been noticing some strange things. The patients seemed more agitated than usual. They weren't as well-rested. Sometimes they had strange moments of confusion. I wasn't able to put it all together at first, but then I started to suspect..."

Doubt clouded Frankie's face, making him drop his eyes and chew his lips. The table was shaking so bad I thought the silverware would bounce right onto the floor. I leaned forward, placing a firm hand on Frankie's forearm. "I've seen things, too," I said. His jittering stopped. "I've seen him. The man in the nightmares. I've seen him myself and I know he's real." I leaned back, but the expression on Frankie's face wasn't one of relief. He looked perplexed.

"What are you talking about?" he asked.

I blinked, mouth opening and closing like a fish. *If he doesn't know about John Albert,* I mused, *then what's he talking about?* Quickly, I recalibrated, changing the direction of the conversation. "The...sleepwalking," I said, opting now to avoid any mention of John Albert until Frankie did. The last thing I needed was for him to think I was losing it. "It's happened to me. The other night when I woke up, I wasn't in my room. I'd never done that before. That's what you were looking for, right? Evidence that the patients were...I don't know, doing weird shit in their sleep?"

Frankie blew out a puff of air and rubbed a hand over his face. "Wow, man. I have no idea what you're talking about. That's not why I put the cameras in the rooms. It had nothing to do with sleepwalking."

I held my hands up, imploring. "Then what were you looking for?"

Frankie glanced around the coffee shop before leaning forward and lowering his voice. "It's Camille." he said.

Now it was my turn to look confused. I gave my head a little shake my mouth drawing open into a small *o*. "Camille? What about her?"

"I noticed her spending a lot of time in some of the patients' rooms. And when I'd go see that patient later, they seemed kind of fucked up. Like, they seemed drugged but also in pain. They were loopy, you know? So one night I decided to ask Camille about it, see if she noticed anything. I followed her into Mr. Paulson's room. She was acting weird, like I had interrupted her. She got real agitated and told me to knock before I came into the room, which I thought was also weird, because I did knock. I always knock. Anyway, she got upset and stormed out of the room and Mr. Paulson tried to say something to me, but he couldn't get the words out, like he was too weak. But here's the thing." Frankie cleared his throat, fingers drumming loudly on the table. "He looked fucking scared, man. Terrified. And you know Mr. Paulson. That dude ain't scared of shit."

I nodded. Mr. Paulson wasn't exactly a lightweight in that department. Even when he'd described seeing the 'spider man' in his room, he hadn't been afraid. Mostly just annoyed.

"But it was more than that. He looked terrified, but also..." A cloud passed over his face and his mouth pulled into a frown at the memory. "I don't know. I don't know how to describe it. But I just became suspicious of her. It was just a feeling I had. But I know a feeling isn't evidence, so..."

Now, Frankie pulled his phone out of his pocket. He

tapped it a few times before handing it to me. "It'll make more sense if you see the video for yourself."

I hit play and hunched over the phone. In the video, Camille was bustling around a woman's room. Straightening curtains, fluffing pillows, things like that. I couldn't quite make out who the patient was. Camille had a satchel strapped diagonally across her torso. That was strange. We weren't supposed to carry personal belongings into the patients' rooms, and a satchel was not part of our uniform.

Camille opened her bag and withdrew something from it, placing it on the patient's night table. I showed Frankie the phone. "What's that?"

Frankie shook his head, his expression growing more agitated. "I don't know. Keep watching."

With my breath caught in my throat, I continued to watch the video. Camille laid a hand on the woman's forearm and then stepped backward, both of her arms lifted upward as if in prayer. It seemed innocuous enough. Weird, maybe, but innocent.

But that's where the innocence ended.

After a moment, the video became hazy around the bed, like there was something wrong with the recording, or like a light source in the room was causing a halo effect. But then, slowly, I realized that what I was seeing wasn't poor video quality; it was a cloud. No, not a cloud. Mist. Pink mist.

The mist grew thicker and redder, blooming until it took up almost the whole frame. Then, Camille moved her hands, both at once, almost as though directing a band. The mist shifted form, coming together in a long, liquid stream that danced in the air. The patient's mouth widened in a silent scream of agony. Again, Camille waved her hands, and the liquid followed her movement, flowing through the air until it found the object she'd placed on the nightstand. As the liquid filled the object, its shape became evident. It was a test tube rack filled with vials.

And the vials were filling up with *blood*.

My eyes flew wide in horror as the ancestral gift of clear thinking took hold of me, whispering answers in my ears, forcing me to draw connections between everything I'd observed. "Jesus Christ, Frankie," I breathed, tapping the video to pause it. "Do you know what this is? Do you know what we're looking at?"

Frankie shook his head. "I have no fucking clue, man. No fucking clue."

I swallowed around the lump in my throat. "We're watching Camille perform a blood siphon ritual." I pressed my fingertips to my eyelids. "Camille is a blood mage."

FRANKIE SCREWED UP HIS FACE, not understanding. "A *what*?"

I puffed out my cheeks, wracking my brain for the best way to explain. "There're many kinds of magic in the world, and many kinds of people who can practice it. Some magic wielders, like me, are born with it. Others, like mages, learn their magic." When Frankie's eyes didn't glaze over, I pressed on. "Every magic is unique. I, for example, can manipulate the death current. Animages can manipulate animal spirits." I thought of John Albert and shuddered. "Mages usually get powers from the aether—but some mages amplify their magic using the so-called humors, or the liquids of the body: yellow bile, black bile, phlegm, and blood." I gestured to the phone. "Camille apparently opted for blood."

I covered my mouth with my hands, staring in stark

disbelief as I trembled with the realization. "She's siphoning blood from that patient and storing it in those vials." Speaking the words aloud helped me form a picture of what was happening. But the picture was incomplete. What was Camille using the blood for? Why did she need it? What was the end goal?

"So she's stealing their blood to use in a ritual? She could have just drawn their blood if that's all she wanted, right?"

I shook my head. "Margaret would notice if her patients had needle marks, even small ones. Plus, it would take forever. No, this way is easier. Safer. It—"

"But wouldn't that kill them? I mean, they're old and weak. And that's a lot of blood."

I tapped *Play*, and Frankie came over to my side of the table so we could watch the video together. Camille pulled blood from her victim until all the vials were filled, and *still* she pulled. Frankie was right. The patient couldn't lose much more blood. So what was Camille doing?

The blood cloud continued to grow until the patient—I now recognized her as Mrs. Lao—lost consciousness. From what I could see, Camille had already taken around fifteen percent of Mrs. Lao's blood. Much more and that old woman would die.

Then, something happened. Camille gathered all the airborne blood into a cluster, suspending it in the air as she leaned forward, her face inches from Mrs. Lao's. Her back was to the camera, and I cursed, wishing I had a better angle.

More, I wished I could *feel* what was happening in that room.

Then, after a moment, she backed away. She lifted her hands once more and the floating glob of blood began to shrink and color slowly returned to Mrs. Lao's face.

Then Camille packed up her vials, tucked them into her bag, and slipped from the room.

The video clip ended there. I handed Frankie the phone, my hands shaking. "So?" he asked, expectant. "What do we do now?"

I propped my chin in my hand. "You could take it to the police," I said. "Practicing blood magic is a crime."

But Frankie sucked his teeth. "Nobody believes in that shit anymore, Kezia. This looks like some kind of magic show trick, you know? They'd laugh me out of the station."

I couldn't argue with that. "Give me a couple days," I suggested. "I want to know what she's *using* all that blood for."

Frankie shuddered as he leaned back in his chair. "She's like a vampire," he said.

I shook my head, recoiling. "The difference is vampires are not real and blood mages are."

We both sat in silence for a long time. We replayed the video over and over again, partially out of disbelief and partially out of, I admit it, morbid curiosity. The last few times I watched the video, I ignored the cloud of blood that formed around Mrs. Lao and focused instead on her face. On the horror that I saw there. The fear.

How many patients had Camille done this to? And for how long?

"I need to see her do this in person," I said finally, getting to my feet and fishing a ten-dollar bill from my purse. I placed it on the table. "That's the only way we're going to understand this for sure."

Frankie gawped, disbelieving. "And how are you going to do that?"

I ran a hand over my hair. "Only one way I can think of."

I GOT into my car and drove immediately to Necro Sis. When Opal saw me, her smile faded to a frown, and her brow creased in worry. "Hey, you look like you seen a ghost. That third-eye tea fuck you up or what?"

Instead of an answer, I took Opal by the hand and led her away from the other customers. When I was relatively sure no one would overhear us, I licked my lips and crossed my arms over my chest. "Hey, I need a favor. I know you're not really big on handing out actual spells to people. But I need some help." I scratched my head and looked around, trying to summon the courage. "What you got that can turn me invisible?"

Opal's eyes darted around the store. She looked as nervous as a whore in church. "What are you talking about?" she asked, her voice pitching an octave too high.

"Listen, Opal. I really do need your help. I'm not doing anything illegal or immoral, I swear."

Opal's expression softened. "I known you for a long time. You don't need to tell me that."

"Good. So then please believe me when I say I don't want to drag you into this, but I do need your help. So what you got? Minor incantation? Cantrip? Ritual? Enchanted fucking necklace?" When Opal still looked dubious, I let a quiver seep into my voice. "Something bad is going down at the hospice. Somebody's been using blood magic on the patients. I need to find out why."

Now, Opal's eyes went wide as the color drained from her face. "Your aunt is there, right?"

I nodded, biting my lower lip. "So now you understand how serious this is."

Opal's nostrils flared as she once again glanced around the shop. Finally, she beckoned for me to follow her. I assumed we were going to head into the back, where she kept the really good enchanted stuff. But instead, we headed right back to her shelves of herbs.

She plucked three different glass containers from the wall. One blend was labeled pregnancy tea, another breakfast of champions, and the last had no label. She pulled the plastic scooper from a drawer and doled out small scoops from each container into a baggie. Then, she beckoned for me to follow her into the back.

I had never been behind Opal's curtains before, and I wasn't sure what to expect. Part of me hoped to find the walls lined with ancient grimoires or perhaps bottles of dead, floating things, or maybe candles that lit themselves and never went out.

Her office had none of those things. Just filing cabinets, dusty boxes, a broken chair and an ancient cathode monitor.

Opal fumbled through a few drawers before finding what she was looking for. It was an ordinary amethyst hanging from a silver chain. She held the pendant over the bag of tea with her eyes closed. She muttered an incantation, the words of which I couldn't quite make out. After a moment, both the pendant and the bag of tea began to glow with a soft lavender light.

The glow didn't last long, however, and I must've looked disappointed, because Opal chuckled as she pressed the tea into my hands. "There you go," she said. "Custom blended invisibili-tea." She laughed at her own pun, and I tucked the blend into a pocket as I rolled my eyes. "The way the enchantment works is this: brew the tea the same way as the third-eye tea I gave you a few days ago. Let it sit for 3 to 4 minutes before drinking it. The effect takes about 30 to 45 minutes to take hold, and will last for almost an hour. But do understand," she said, her tone growing serious, "ain't no such thing as true invisibility. Anyone who is looking for you or knows you're there will see you. It's really more of an... overlooking tea. It makes you dim. Not worthy of notice. So, if you're walking into a dangerous situation, be careful. But I probably don't need to tell you that," Opal finished.

"I really appreciate this," I said. "How much do I owe you?"

Opal clucked her tongue against her teeth. "More than you got on you, I promise you that. I'll send you a bill."

I grimaced, but it was only fair. If I had Opal's gift, I'd charge an arm and a leg for it, too. "Thanks, Opal. I'll see you soon."

She grinned. "Don't threaten me."

8

CAMILLE WAS SCHEDULED for a night shift the next evening. Although Big Ginny tried to convince me to mind my business and let the police handle it, there was no way I was letting Camille get away with whatever evil she was planning. Around ten o'clock, I brewed myself a batch of the invisibility tea, and then, thinking better of it, added a couple pinches of the third-eye tea as well. My inner pharmacist shouted that I probably shouldn't mix magical potions, but to hell with it. I needed all the help I could get. After all, the safety of our patients was up to me. I needed to know what I was up against. I needed to know what *they* were up against.

The blended effect of the tea took a while to come on. But after about 45 minutes, I felt the change. I sensed things I was normally unaware of: my heartbeat, the pulsing of my lungs, the undulation of my aura. I also heard Big Ginny's breathing down the hall, the crickets outside our door chirping mercilessly, even the slither of shadows across our meager lawn. If I listened carefully, I could hear the gentle beginning of an earthquake trying to rumble its way to the surface.

With my heightened senses, I got into my car and made the drive over to the hospice. When I arrived, there were few cars in the lot. I slipped into the lobby, walking past Michael who didn't even glance up at me. The tea was working. Now I just needed to find Camille and hope she did something bloody and evil before the spell wore off.

I eventually found her in Mrs. Olson's room. I pushed the door open, stepping in quietly, letting the door click softly shut behind me. Camille hadn't seen me enter. Still, I kept to the shadows, my back pressed against the wall as I slithered into a corner of the room where I had a complete view of what Camille was doing. When I'd seen her activities on Frankie's video, I'd only been able to see her back. Now, I could see everything.

The beginning of her ritual was the same as what we had seen on the video. She placed a rack of glass vials on Mrs. Olson's nightstand before siphoning the old woman's blood into the air and filling the vials with the dark red liquid. The smell of blood and iron was thick in the air, and it was all I could do not to retch. Seeing that mist of blood on video was one thing; seeing it, feeling it, hearing it, and smelling it in real life was another. The look on Camille's face, too, was horrifying. She looked enchanted, like a woman besotted with a new lover. Her glee was evident and sickening and I clenched my hands at my sides, forcing myself to stay rooted to the spot. I wanted to run over and knock her to the ground, put my hands around her neck and throttle her until she passed out. Everything she was doing was so contrary to what I believed in, to what I had been trained in.

But I stood my ground and waited.

That's when I noticed it. The thickening of the death current. With the help of the third-eye tea, I could see it with my eyes: a slow, steady pulse of violet energy that circulated throughout the room. It grew thicker and brighter around Mrs. Olson, pressing against her skin. After a short while, a second energy appeared, and I knew that Mrs. Olson's time was drawing near. I felt the change in my hands first: the cold throb that started in my palms and radiated out to my fingertips. But then I saw it. Unlike the death current, this second energy wasn't calm and peaceful. It was bright green and effervescent, and suddenly I felt it all over my body. Not just in my hands, but along my skin, in the roots of my teeth, in the marrow of my bones. And it wasn't cold—no, it was joy. It felt like bubbles and laughter and cajoling. It felt like applause, like cheerleading, like carbonated beverages. It was such a strange sensation that for a minute I couldn't quite understand what was happening.

But then I took my eyes off Camille and looked at Mrs. Olson and I understood. Mrs. Olson was surrounded by mortic energy. It was time for her to pass.

I held my breath, not daring to breathe. Camille had finished siphoning Mrs. Olson's blood and was now holding the excess in the air. What the hell was she doing with it?

As the suspended blood glistened, Camille leaned forward, pressing her face into the vibrant green mortic energy that had appeared only moments ago. And then her mouth began to move as though she were whispering.

The change was almost imperceptible. If Opal hadn't gifted me with clear thinking, I'm sure I would have missed it. Even the third-eye tea wouldn't have been enough.

But as Camille's mouth worked, two things happened at once. The first was that the cloud of blood shrank as Camille reversed her siphon, sending the blood back into Mrs. Olson's body.

The second was that Mrs. Olson's mortic energy began to shrink.

I gasped only a little, still afraid that if I made too much noise, I would draw attention to myself. But Camille didn't notice me. She was ecstatic, like a woman in the middle of orgasm. She took deep, glorious breaths, color rising in her cheeks as she sucked in the neon green miasma.

But she wasn't really *breathing* Mrs. Olson's mortic energy, was she?

No, I knew better than that. She was *consuming* it.

Suddenly, everything made sense. Camille wasn't just a blood mage. She was a necrophage. A death eater. Someone who consumed the death of others to keep her own death at bay. She brought her victims close to death by draining their blood and then, when their mortic energy appeared, she devoured it. That's why she needed all that blood— it allowed her to perform this magic, this arcane necrophagy, an art no one practiced anymore. Consuming mortic energy kept her young—it kept her alive.

My mind flashed back to the night in the parking lot, the night Camille's dog had died. She looked wan, underfed. The collar of her scrubs had slipped down a bony shoulder, revealing a dark smudge underneath her collarbone. I remembered thinking it looked like flaking shoe polish.

But it wasn't shoe polish. It was blood. As a blood mage, Camille needed that reagent on her skin to perform her rituals. It explained the obnoxious rose perfume, too. The perfume covered the smell of blood.

The realization rendered me dizzy, and I swayed under the weight of the implications. How many shifts had Camille and I spent together? How close had I been to another person's blood smeared across her skin? The thought was disgusting and infuriating. Frankie was right. She *was* like a vampire. She didn't have fangs and she could walk in sunlight, but this woman was just as monstrous as those fantastical beasts. Maybe worse.

If I'd had any sense at all, I would have dipped out of the room and called the police right then and there. But now that I understood what Camille was doing, I was filled with a rage so bright and blinding that I couldn't think straight. I was all fight, no flight.

I was in the mood to *square up with this bitch.*

"Camille."

My voice startled her out of her trance, and she yelped as she spun around, her eyes going wide in the dark. The last of the blood that had been floating in the air splashed down onto the floor, splattering against the bed and walls. She took a step backward, her newly flushed cheeks now growing pale at being discovered.

"Where did you come from?" she breathed, whipping her head back and forth as though trying to see through the shadows.

I stepped forward, taking a perverse joy in watching her shrink back from me. "I can't believe it took me this long to see it," I said, hands balled at my sides. "You're not some kind of charismatic negotiator. You don't talk the elderly back from death. You consume their mortic energy. You use the force that's supposed to allow them to peacefully die and you feed on it yourself." I swallowed, my entire body shaking. "Mrs. Olson is *suffering,*" I shot, my voice quivering with emotion. "She's been in terrible pain for *weeks*. How can you do that?

How can you deny her the right to die and end that suffering?"

Camille's nostrils flared. She held her hands out, palms up, pleading. "Kezia, you don't understand," she said. "These people *need* me. They're not ready to go."

"Like hell they aren't," I said, taking another step toward her. Two. "You don't get to decide that. You can't—"

She was so much faster than I could have expected. She leapt at me, her momentum carrying us crashing into the wall. I stretched my fingers for her eyes, to claw at her and take her out, but she was faster than I was. She threw me to the ground, pulling something from the satchel strapped across her body. I hardly even had time to register the hypodermic needle before she plunged it into my thigh.

Stunned, I stumbled backward, my vision going in and out. She'd hit me with some kind of tranquilizer. I should have had minutes before the full effects took hold, but the combination of magic tea blends must have sped up the process. Within seconds, my head started to feel fuzzy.

The world slipped underwater. My vision clouded and my body went slack. Camille hovered close to my face, eyes peering into mine, watching me fight for consciousness. Her breath smelled too sweet, like rotting fruit. She was whispering an incantation, and I tried to fight against her, but my body was made of lead, too heavy to move. But as my eyes fluttered closed, my clear thinking gift blazed to life, and I heard my own voice, wiser and sharper, whisper, *The spell she's casting is for forgetting. She's laying words on you to make you forget.*

But I won't let that happen.

And before I could fight my way out of the deepening chasm, I slipped into unconsciousness.

I woke up about 30 minutes later, feeling discombobulated and pissed off. As I came back into my body, I saw Mrs. Olson watching me, her eyes wide with fear. Camille probably forgot to enchant the old woman. I whispered apologies to Mrs. Olson, promising her I'd fix everything. As I climbed to my feet, I remembered Michael saying Jennifer had passed out in Mr. Bennett's room. Jennifer had surmised that she'd passed out from low blood sugar, but now I suspected that she'd caught Camille performing illegal blood magic, been tranquilized, and had her memory of the event magicked away.

That pissed me off even more. Jennifer was annoying, but harmless. She didn't deserve that.

The anger cleared the rest of the fog from my brain. I searched the hospice for Camille, but she'd gone. Scared that she might try to hit me where it would hurt most, I hurried out to my car and hauled ass back home. Back to Big Ginny.

I stormed into the house to find Big Ginny in the living room was a bowl of popcorn watching an old movie. But when she saw the look on my face, her brow furrowed in worry. "What's wrong? Where you been?"

I brushed my hands together. "No time. Come on. We got work to do." I said.

Big Ginny didn't question me. She set the bowl of popcorn to the side and followed me into the kitchen. I glanced at the clock. 11:30. It was better to do a binding at midnight. The crossroads between one day and another was a powerful time, and we needed all the advantages we could get. The work we needed to do to bind Camille from doing harm to anyone else would require a lot of energy.

"You gonna tell me what's going on here?"

I set my hands on my hips. "We got to put a bitch in her place."

I explained everything as I pulled the necessary ingredients from the cabinets and got the altar set up. I told her about Frankie's video and the blood siphoning and the death eating and getting drugged. Big Ginny listened with rapt attention, her eyes as wide as saucers. "A real blood mage," she said. "And a necrophage at that! I've only ever heard stories about them. Never met one in real life."

"I know," I said, clenching my jaw. "It's the kind of thing you read about in a horror story, but you never expect to see for yourself. Can you imagine? She eats their death energy," I mused. "I wonder how long she's been doing it for."

"A little over a hundred years."

The voice startled me so bad I screamed and backed into my grandmother who toppled into a chair. I searched for the source of the voice, but there wasn't anyone else in the room.

It was Big Ginny who noticed it first. She held up a shaking hand, pointing a crooked finger at a shadow creeping along the floor. "Cricket," she whispered.

I followed her gaze, my breath hitching in my throat. The cricket was looking at us, and as I stared back at it, I sensed more than saw the silhouette of a man with dark skin and white hair.

John Albert.

"What are you doing here?" I stammered. "What do you want? I thought I—"

"You do too much thinking and not enough at the same time," he snapped. The biting reprimand felt like a slap in the face. "Who you think been watching out for them folks? Who you think kept that fly from causing harm? Why you think them folks finally up and died, all six in a row? Heh," he grunted with a slow shake of his head. "You shoulda figured it by now. You got that glow on you," he said, pointing toward his forehead. "That clear thinking gift. Too bad you ain't had it sooner."

I squeezed my eyes shut, my brow twisting with under-standing—too little and too late. "You were *protecting* them," I breathed. "That's why you were in their rooms. Keeping Camille from getting to them. The web you were knitting was for her. To keep her away." I swallowed around the lump in my throat. "And I cut the webs down," I whispered.

"Yeah, you stupid all right," John Albert agreed, smacking his lips. "And you was so proud of yasself! I thought you had brains but you too busy believing everything you heard about me." It didn't take a genius to know he was talking about the stories I'd heard from Big Ginny. "Yes, I was keeping them folks safe. That evil woman couldn't get to them, not with my webs up. Didn't you see her face? How colorless she got when she couldn't get close enough to suck them dry? You shoulda known when you looked at her something was wrong!"

"I *did* know," I shot back, remembering how gaunt and pale Camille had looked earlier, "but she said it was because her dog…" I shook myself, heaving a sigh as I wondered now if Camille ever *had* a dog. The whole scenario might have been a lie. "I didn't know what she was then. And I thought *you* were the one keeping Aunt Fat from passing over."

John Albert growled. "What would I do that for?"

"Spite," I said. "To keep her from her child."

Again, John Albert smacked his lips. "Y'all been listening too long to old wives' tales."

"You could have told me what you were up to!" I snapped, real anger edging into my voice. "You could have said some-thing instead of letting me think—"

"I ain't owed you no explanation!" he said, a wet laugh rounding out the words. "Who you think you is? You still wet behind the ears! You ain't nothing! I ain't gotta explain myself to you. Heh."

Big Ginny kept silent as she continued her preparation for the binding ritual, lighting candles and incense and setting the makeshift altar with chicken bones, playing cards, Florida water, scraps of cloth, cords, matches.

"I'm sorry I doubted your intentions," I said to John Albert. My apology seemed to do the trick; his face softened, and his posture relaxed. "But now we really need to get to work."

I had turned my attention to the kitchen altar to begin the binding ritual when my phone rang.

Big Ginny and I both froze. My phone never rang, and certainly not at this hour. When I glanced down, I didn't recognize the number. I almost thumbed the phone to silent, but Big Ginny nodded toward the device with a grim look on her face. "Better answer that," she said.

I lifted the phone to my ear. "Hello?"

The voice on the other end was hurried and tinted with fear. "Oh my God, Kezia, I was so afraid you wouldn't answer." It took me a moment to place the voice out of context. I'd never spoken to Jennifer on the phone before. "I went to see that woman like you told me to. Opal? The necromancer? She gave me a gift."

I squeezed my eyes shut and tilted my head back in frustration. "Jennifer, it's late. Maybe we can talk—"

"No, don't interrupt. This is important. The gift I received was clairvoyance. And I just saw a vision that you need to know about."

I leaned my weight against the counter, my head swimming. "I saw a woman going into your aunt's room," she said.

"And I heard Ms. Jamerson screaming in pain as the woman stood over her bed. I couldn't tell who the woman was, though it kind of looked like Camille." She paused, and I found that I couldn't speak, my voice trapped in my throat. "I looked at the clock. The vision happens at 12:15. I know it's not much time, and I'm sorry about that. But I just had the vision. You need to go over there. Right now. Before the screaming starts."

I glanced at the clock. It was almost midnight now. With my heart racing, I clutched the phone tighter. "Thank you," I breathed.

I hung up the phone to find Big Ginny and John Albert staring at me, waiting to hear what I'd learned. But I spoke directly to the apparition in my kitchen. "It's Aunt Fat," I breathed, though I had a feeling he already knew this. "She's in trouble. Can you get over there? Can you go now and protect her? There's not much time. She—"

"Can't," he interrupted, giving a soft shrug of a shoulder. "They done exterminated over there. No horses for me to ride. It's too late for me to help now. It's all on you."

I bit back a curse as I grabbed Big Ginny by the arm. "We need to go. Now."

9

WITH BIG GINNY IN TOW, I barreled through the streets of Los Angeles, pressing my car and my nerves to their limits. We had so little time to intercept Camille before she did something unforgivable.

Plus, I wanted to give Big Ginny enough time to say goodbye.

I pushed harder on the gas.

When we finally arrived, Big Ginny and I hurried through the parking lot and through the front doors. I darted into the kitchen, my clear thinking gift compelling me to grab the tin I'd given Jennifer, and dashed back out to the lobby. I glanced at my watch. 12:10. I took Big Ginny by the hand as I led her toward Aunt Fat's room. The fluorescent lights flickered overhead as I pushed open the door and stepped inside.

The smell of death hung heavy in the air.

The door clicked closed, and Aunt Fat's eyes fluttered open. When her gaze landed on Big Ginny, a smile spread over her face. I retreated to the edge of the room, allowing the two cousins to share an intimate moment in private. Big Ginny leaned in, planting a firm kiss on her cousin's cheek. When they separated, I saw tears in both their eyes.

"It's getting close, ain't it?" Big Ginny asked.

Aunt Fat tried to answer, but her throat was too dry. I came forward with a jar of Vaseline and smeared a thin film over her lips and gums to give her some comfort as she tried to speak. I saw the gratefulness in her eyes, tugging on my heartstrings. Tears sprung unbidden to my eyes. "We love you so much," I said.

Aunt Fat smiled. "I know," she said.

Big Ginny took her cousin's hands in her own and began to sing, a bluesy, country melody with the lyrics of her favorite Psalm. Psalm 130. I retreated further into the shadows, making myself as unobtrusive as possible. This moment wasn't about me. Even in death, I could still visit Aunt Fat. That was one of the advantages of being a natural-born necromancer. Death for me just turned a local conversation into a long-distance one. I could see Aunt Fat for many years to come. But Big Ginny couldn't.

Big Ginny's song had barely faded into silence when the door creaked open. I glanced at the clock, my pulse quickening and my mouth running dry. 12:15. That bitch was right on time.

Camille stepped into the room, letting the door click closed behind her. For a moment, she simply stared at Big Ginny. She hadn't been expecting company.

I waited, choosing my opening move carefully. Camille took a few steps toward my grandmother before stopping, hands on her hips when she said, "Are you looking for Kezia? I think I saw her headed toward the nurse's station just a few moments ago. You might be able to catch her if you leave now. You wouldn't want her to miss her aunt's death."

Taking this as my cue, I stepped from the shadows, and when I emerged into the light, Camille's eyes went wide. "Oh," she said, donning her characteristic sweet smile. "I didn't see you there. I was just coming to administer Ms. Jamerson's medication."

I balled my hands into fists. "You can cut the bullshit," I said. "Your spell didn't work. I remember everything."

Camille stepped forward, her gaze flitting between me, Big Ginny, and Aunt Fat, whose eyes were wide with fear in the darkness. Camille's smile was cool and calculated when she said, "Then I guess we'll both do what we have to."

She moved so quickly. She darted towards me and knocked Big Ginny to the ground as I dodged her attack. My grandmother yelped as she landed with a thud. At her age, taking a fall like that could be damn near fatal. The fury that ignited in me rose to my skin like fire, but I held my ground. I knew Camille probably had another needle waiting. I couldn't risk getting close until I was ready to make my move. But I also couldn't let her get close to Big Ginny.

I worked at the lid inside my pocket as I backed away from Camille, keeping my grandmother in my peripheral vision. "This stops tonight, Camille. No more magic. No more pain and suffering. You do know that, right?"

"Why are you doing this?" she asked. "Your aunt doesn't have to die tonight. I can stop that from happening! I can make sure she lives long enough to say goodbye to the people who love her. Long enough to make her apologies to everyone she's ever wronged. Long enough to know that her life has meant something. Why would you deprive her of that? What am I doing that's so wrong? Everyone is afraid of death! I can take that fear away!"

"You're unnatural," I said through a clenched jaw. "Everything that lives dies. That's the natural order of the universe. Yes, death is sad for those left behind, but it's not sad for the dead! It's joyful for those who move on! Why are *you* so afraid of death, Camille?"

Camille shook her head, her perfect ponytail coming loose, her edges beginning to fray. "I'm not afraid of anything!" she snapped. "But why should I die? Why should I have to let...*my* body...*rot*..."

"Don't you see what you've become? Preying on old, helpless people? Your body is intact, but your insides rotted a long time ago." I stepped closer to her, adrenaline pushing me forward. "You could've done so much more with your life, but you traded what you had for this ridiculous pursuit of eternal youth. It will never make you happy. You'll spend every moment pursuing another day, another hour, another minute. And you'll never find satisfaction."

But Camille wasn't paying any attention to me. I could see all over her face that she was only calculating her next move. And she wasn't going to try tranquilizing me again.

If she got a chance, Camille would kill me.

That realization was all the conviction I needed.

I pounced. I threw myself into her, the momentum carrying both of us to the ground. I caught an elbow in the face; I retaliated with a fist into her teeth. Blood trickled down my knuckles. We tussled on the ground, me on top, then her. We slashed each other's faces, gouged toward each other's eyes. I heard Big Ginny sobbing in the background. I thrust Camille off of me long enough to reach once more into my pocket, the lid finally off the honey powder.

My clear thinking gift surged to life once more, confirming a memory I had of Camille, eyes unfocused, as she said with casual indifference, "I'm allergic to honey."

I'm allergic to honey.

I prayed that allergy was deadly.

I plunged my fingers into the tin, withdrawing a handful of sticky powder. With a snarling grunt, I smashed it into Camille's face, grinding the powder into her eyes, her nostrils, her lips.

Camille squealed and bucked her hips as she began to choke. Her eyes went wide as she clawed at her throat, her wheezing growing harsher and more frenzied. With her eyes bulging and her tongue peeking out from between her lips, she wheezed, "What did you do?"

I scrambled to my feet and backed away from her as she lay on the ground, spasming in anaphylactic shock. I helped my grandmother onto her feet and turned her around so that her back was to the horror happening behind her. Big Ginny didn't need to see that.

My grandmother trembled as she sat on the edge of the bed. With tears streaming down her face, Big Ginny placed her hands one final time on her cousin's cheeks. "I love you so much, Fat. You've been such a joy in my life."

Aunt Fat's chin trembled. "Is it my time? Is Jinabbott…is Jinabbott gonna…?"

Big Ginny shushed her cousin, brushing sweat from her brow. "Never was John Albert keeping you here, sugar," she said. "He was here to protect you from evil. But the evil been dealt with. It's safe for you, now." She paused, her voice hitching in her throat. "Charmaine's waiting for you on the other side."

Aunt Fat didn't respond, but the tears that shone in her

eyes said everything her body couldn't. Big Ginny kissed her once more before sitting upright and beginning to pray. "May the Lord be kind to you as you pass into the light to find Him on the other side," she prayed through trembling lips. "May you find peace and comfort in the warmth of his eternal love."

Both women intoned together, "Amen."

I came forward, somber, and clasped Aunt Fat's hands in my own. "Rest in power, auntie," I whispered.

The energy in the room changed. The death current thrummed and my hands buzzed, letting me know it was time for my aunt to pass. And though I couldn't see it with my physical eyes, I sensed my aunt's mortic energy shimmering into being—I smelled baby oil and moth balls and Avon lipstick. I choked back a sob, recognizing these scents for what they were—the beginning of my aunt's final transformation. I watched as Aunt Fat's biological processes slowed. First her breathing stopped. Then her heart. Then the electric currents of her brain. Then at last, her vital spark dissipated, and her soul slipped from her body, released finally from the bonds of earth as it slipped through the veil to find comfort and peace with her ancestors on the other side.

Big Ginny let out a wail and began to sob just as I turned around to find Camille prone on the ground, glass eyes turned up to the ceiling, but those eyes didn't see anything.

Camille, too, lay dead.

BY THE TIME the first responders appeared on the scene, Camille's corpse had already aged. When she died, Camille looked to be perhaps in her late 20s. But now, the corpse on the floor was desiccated, cadaverous eyes peering out from behind white, milky cataracts. Her mouth, too, was sunken, as the teeth one by one vanished from her mouth. Her tongue blackened. The skin became thin and translucent, revealing the skeleton beneath.

John Albert was right. By the looks of her, Camille was well over 100 years old. She'd been keeping people alive for a very long time.

As the night wound down, I found myself sitting outside on the same bench I had shared with Camille just recently. Margaret was occupying the space now, her arms wrapped around her as she shuddered against a thin breeze. Evenings in Los Angeles were often cool, but I knew it wasn't the cold getting to her. It was the shock of everything that had happened right under her nose.

"Are you okay?" I asked.

Margaret rubbed her face with both hands, then ran her fingers through her hair before answering. She blew out her cheeks in frustration as she shook her head, tears leaking from the corners of her eyes. "I just don't understand how I never saw it." She pressed her chin to her chest, and the tears fell from her eyes into her lap. "The families loved Camille. They loved the way she could extend their time together. It never occurred to me that she was hurting them. That she had to hurt them to do what she did. I only saw the gift. I never saw what it cost."

I folded my arms over my chest and leaned my head back, taking in the meager starlight. "See, that's the thing. Where you're wrong, I mean. It was never a gift. From the very beginning, everything Camille did was evil."

Margaret's expression was confused when she turned her face to me. "How's that?"

Our thighs pressed together, and I was grateful for

Margaret's warmth. The evening's events had already left me cold. I needed to go home and sleep, but even that was still a long way off. But at least I could take comfort in human nearness. Human contact. Something I had so little of in my private life.

"Everybody has a right to die peacefully," I said. "That's part of what we're doing here. In hospice. It's part of what drew me into thanatology in the first place. I know there's something else beyond this world. I've seen it. That's one of the few advantages I have as a necromancer, one of the reasons I'm not afraid of death. Because I know what happens next. I know that we are reunited with our ancestors, our history, our lineage. It's the completion of a cycle. And every person has a right to that. Especially when they're suffering. Camille took that away from those people. Sure, she gave families extra time, but did they really need it?" I sighed, giving my head an angry shake. "Maybe they did need that time, but they shouldn't have. We all need to think more seriously about the time we spend with each other when we're all alive. We need to stop relying on these last few minutes to tell people that we love them, or how important they are to us. Why do we wait for death to do that? I don't know why," I admitted. "Maybe we take each other for granted. Maybe we always think we'll have more time."

I returned my gaze to the sky, seeking out the stars. But there were so few. For some reason, this made me sadder than usual. "So anyway, no. You won't convince me that Camille had a gift. Camille was a selfish, evil person taking away the peace due to us to extend her own life. Because she was scared. Scared of what? I don't know. If she'd asked me or any other natural-born necromancer, we could've explained to her that there's nothing to be afraid of. It's not all darkness and cold and loneliness. It's family, acceptance, and deep-seated satisfaction. I could have assuaged her fears." I wiped away a tear that had managed its way down my cheek. I hadn't even known I was crying. "But I don't know. She had held onto that fear for such a long time that maybe it was impossible to quell those worries. In any case, it's over now."

We sat together in silence for a long time. I don't know how late it was when the last person from the shift finally left hospice and the last of the cops got into their patrol vehicles and pulled away. But eventually, Margaret pulled herself to standing, and I followed suit. We stood there for a while staring at each other, little more than strangers, but bound together now by a terrible event that no two people should have to share.

"I learned a lot from you tonight," Margaret said. "Thank you for everything you did. It was ballsy. They could still charge you with something. But at least we have the video. I hope that's enough."

I nodded. "It's not like I really had a choice," I said. "Family protects family. Otherwise, what's the point?"

Margaret nodded. "Yeah. Well, like I said. Thank you." She turned to walk away, but stopped mid-turn, her gaze lifting to meet mine one more time. Her expression softened as she said, as though suddenly remembering, "I'm so sorry for your loss."

I shrugged, offering a soft smile. "No worries. I have every intention of crossing over to visit her tomorrow. I'll tell her you said hello."

WEEKS LATER, long after Big Ginny and I had settled into our normal routines, I was sitting at my altar getting ready to reach out to my mother. The lights were dim, and the incense was lit. With a match in hand I leaned forward to light my ancestor candles. But just as I was about to touch the flame to the wick of the blue candle of my forefathers, I heard a voice in my head.

"Wait."

I looked up, my eyes wide in the darkness, but there was no one there. "Hello?" I asked aloud.

From the corner of my eye, I caught a small movement, a slight undulation of shadow. There, in the corner of my room, was a cricket. And from the cricket's shadow rose the unmistakable form of a man. A man who, by now, I knew well.

I chewed my bottom lip. "John Albert? Is that you?"

His form became clearer now. I saw the dark eyes and weathered skin. He looked older than he had the last time I'd seen him, but also less menacing. His expression was kind as he turned those dark eyes on me, and that full mouth turned up into a smile. "I been waiting on you to visit me," he said.

My brows drew together in confusion. "Me? Why would I do that?"

I heard him sigh as he shook his head. "Thought you'd have figured that by now, too. Don't you think I got nothing to teach you?"

I sucked in a breath, my heart suddenly racing. "You want to pass your magic and memories to me?" I asked. "But we're not even kin. I mean, not really. Not by blood."

John Albert took a few faltering steps toward me, not enough for the light to fall on him. He kept to the shadows and crossed his arms over his chest. "Don't you know nothing about family after all this time? You my kin, all right. Fat's, too. And that candle you about to light shouldn't be dedicated to no faceless forefathers. Ever since Fat passed over, I been watching out for you. And I'll keep on watching out for you. You got a good heart, Kezia, and when you get your Godsend, you'll make an amazing necromancer. All the power and light your kind is supposed to give our community? You'll give it. I'll help you when the time come. Least you can do is call on me when you light them candles."

Warmth bloomed in my chest and spread into my stomach and limbs. A gentle joy that I couldn't quite explain unfolded in my heart, and my eyes grew damp with tears. I'd been searching for my own ancestors, my progenitors whose DNA I shared, for years and years. But here was someone who came to find *me*. Who had claimed *me*.

Who was I to complain?

I nodded and folded my hands in my lap. "Of course I'll light this candle for you," I said. "Papa John Albert," I said trying the words out on my tongue. But they didn't feel quite right. "Papa Jinabbott," I amended. "And Mama Fat." I grinned. Now, that felt right. "You can't possibly know how much that means to me."

John Albert clucked his tongue and gave me a genuine smile. "I might know more than you think. Keep looking for her, now. Keep looking for your mama. Don't you never give up on your Godsend."

I shook my head, letting the tears fall. "I won't. I promise."

"I know you won't. You'll find her. And then you'll have all the magic you need to bring your baby back home."

At the mention of my baby, a fresh sob threatened to quake through my body. How did he know about her? No one outside my family knew the sacrifice I'd had to make as a necromancer without a Godsend.

But then, maybe he was right, and he was my family after all.

I fought back my tears, nodding earnestly. "I'll do everything in my power. I swear. Thank you."

And with that, John Albert melted into the shadows, but not before I saw him smile, his own cheeks damp with joyful tears.

ABOUT THE AUTHOR

Amber Fisher is the author of urban and contemporary fantasy books ranging from sweet and delightful to dark and morbid. She lives in Austin, Texas, in a near-empty house now that her two kids have flown the coop. She would enjoy the silence except her husband is noisy as hell.

Connect with me at: amberfishermedia.com

Facebook at: facebook.com/amberfisherauthor

Twitter: @amberla

Sign up for the newsletter: bit.ly/332eurl

Copyright © 2020 by Amber Fisher

All rights reserved.

No part of this book may be reproduced in any form or by any electronic or mechanical means, including information storage and retrieval systems, without written permission from the author, except for the use of brief quotations in a book review.

Made in United States
North Haven, CT
18 October 2021

10398644R00074